Until
I Decide

T.I. LOWE

My first book, *Lulu's Café*, was published January 12, 2014. To celebrate the 5th anniversary, I wanted to give my reading friends a new book. *Until I Decide* is for each one of you who has cheered me on, laughed with me, and shed a few tears. Thank you.

Books by T.I.LOWE

Lulus Café

The Bleu Streak Series:
Goodbyes & Second Chances
A Bleu Streak Christmas
A Bleu Streak Summer

The Coming Home Again Series:
Coming Home Again
Julia's Journey
A Discovery of Hope

Any Given Moment

The Resolutions Series:
Until I Do
Until I Don't
Until I Decide

The Carolina Coast Series - publish date – 2020:
Driftwood Dreams
Beach Haven
Sea Glass Castle

ACKNOWLEDGMENTS

Thank you, Christina Coryell for all of the advice and work you put into this book. I sure am glad God saw fit to have our writing paths cross and for the friendship that developed from it. Love you, my author sister!

I am grateful for the love and support of my family and friends. My Lowe bunch may not always understand my writing process, but they give me the room needed to get it done and are always the quickest to cheer me on. Bernie, Nate the Great, and Lydia Lu, you are my greatest gift. I love the story God has written for us as a family.

Nate the Great, we are looking at the year you graduate. Proud is not a creative enough word to describe how I feel about you and everything you've achieved with integrity and diligence. My prayer is that you continue to make wise decisions based on your faith in God.

My favs in no particular order—Teresa Moise, Lynn Edge, Sally Anderson, Trina Cooke, Denise Rosenau, and Jennifer Strickland. You ladies are priceless and I appreciate you and your love and your friendship far more than my mere words can describe. Love ya.

Dana McCall Michael and Julie Jobe, thanks ladies for reading an early edition of Until I Decide and giving me your valuable opinions. You are honest and always quick to support me and my stories. I treasure you both.

My blessings go far beyond what's listed. My Savior Jesus Christ is so good to me!

Prologue

The thought of a dead body underneath a crisp white sheet conjured a different image than the reality of the one before me. Perhaps it had been romanticized in a morbid way, skewed by the fictional world of movies and drama series. Neat and tidy, a tag tied with care around the big toe to declare who the body once was and what he can never be again.

There is no tag and there's nothing neat and tidy in the stark, sterile room frigid in both temperature and mood.

Standing on trembling legs that refuse to move closer than about a yard away, my eyes scan the slight form hidden underneath the sheet. It barely makes peaks on the landscape of postmortem. A few faint stains along the edge of the white cloth underscore the situation. It's dire. It's devastating.

"That can't be him." The statement squeaks out over a whisper, very little conviction behind it. I wipe the sheen of sweat collecting on my brow and then slide my palm down the side of my jeans. *He was larger in life than this small, misshapen image of death.*

The medical examiner moves his gloved hand to peel back the not-so crisp white sheet. Instinct screams for me to grasp some self-preservation and look away, but my eyes are glued to the stainless-steel gurney. An end to a part of me. I'm not prepared to face it quite yet.

Can one ever be ready for such a thing?

No. Definitely not.

The sheet shifts to reveal the weight of my new, unwanted reality. Then the room shifts abruptly with it. Auburn curls slowly come into view. They no longer glisten with golden accents, but are now left matted and dull from tragedy. I suck in a breath and am unable to swallow the sob as the sheet unfolds more, exposing truths I don't want to believe. If it wasn't for the bloat and discoloration of his skin and the odd concaved shape on the left side of his forehead, I could almost pretend he's just sleeping. If only he was snoring that whistling tune of his. How many times had I teased him about that? I'd give anything to have that noise back and keeping me awake at night.

Surrounded by the sharp tinges of chemicals and regret, the white-tiled room around me sways severely and blurs.

"I'm going to throw—"

The declaration doesn't beat his reaction to the finish line. The medical examiner has exceptionally quick reflexes, because a stainless-steel bowl catches all of the vile hurt spewing from me. When the retching stops producing anything more than dry heaves, he leads me to a chair. The cool metal on my overheated back reminds me I dashed out of the door without covering the tank top I wore to bed. What I would give for one of Beau's sweatshirts at the moment.

My thoughts rewind to the reason I was wearing the tank top in the first place. Beau's sweet phone call earlier, insinuating that it was time to get to work extending our world with a baby. After three years of marriage, with life growing sweeter by the day, we were ready. We'd already discussed name options and had a few wistful conversations about what characteristics we hoped we passed to the baby. Beau's wish list included his green eyes and my black hair. Mine focused on his red curls and my curious gold eyes.

I told Beau I'd wait up for him, but he insisted I go on to bed, preferably wearing a tank top and a pair of boyshorts. We both laughed, because the outfit equaled the finest silk negligee in his opinion. After hanging up, I'd chosen the polka-dot boyshorts, knowing that man would love me in a tater sack.

I almost smile at that thought until an icy shiver skirts along my exposed shoulders. At least I took the time to pull on some jeans before I followed the police officer to the morgue. There's a small hole at the knee. I touch a shaky fingertip to the exposed skin, looking anywhere but at the lifeless body across the room from me. The hanging scale sways in my periphery where I think I knocked into it before getting sick, but I dare not look over for confirmation.

"Is there someone I can call for you?" the older gentleman asks over the pounding in my eardrums.

Heaving a few staggered breaths that burn my throat, I somehow find my voice and rasp, "My husband, please."

The medical examiner sets the bowl down somewhere and returns to kneel beside me. He clears his throat. "Mrs. McCoy…"

We both know what he wants to clarify. The fact that my husband will never answer a phone again. A long stretch of time slips by before I pass my phone to him and then rub a palm to my chest while I watch him look at me expectantly.

"Chase McCoy, my brother-in-law," I explain after snapping out of the daze. "He's the closest family I have in Tennessee." My shock keeps me from fully grasping the impact this is going to have on Chase's life as well. Losing his baby brother and only sibling.

A few minutes wobble along, marked by a wall clock ticking somewhere in the room, before he speaks. "Yes, Mr. McCoy, I have your sister-in-law Bellamy with me…"

I tune the rest of it out, not wanting to hear the replay. How Beau was on his way home from a youth evangelism conference up in Nashville. How a drunk driver took what he had no right to take. My husband's life. Our life. Our dreams.

Chapter One

Two years later...

Lee Sutton

Absolute darkness holds me for longer than necessary. I fight against it, but it keeps slipping back over me like a sticky film. When I blink, a few stray stars come into focus. I stare at them until the moon and a piercing pain catch my attention. It's coming at me from all different directions, so it's hard to pinpoint exactly where the damage is. The film slips back into place before I can make heads or tails of it.

Angry beats from a heavy metal song scream from the speakers of my bike, bringing me back to the side of the road where I'm sprawled out. If I could move my arm, I'd pat myself on the back. I'm boss when it comes to building a sick bike. This one that just got up to 180 mph is no exception. Good thing I let off the throttle before that last switchback...

I try to take a deep breath, but a pinch in my side halts it just as I get a whiff of smoke in the air. Between the smoke and the rushing sound of a waterfall somewhere nearby, something registers in my jumbled brain and reminds me of a camping trip I went on with my old man and Tommy before my little brother became too sick. I'd call Pop and we'd reminisce about the good ole days before our home life went to crap, if I could find my phone. He wouldn't answer anyway.

I make the mistake of trying to move again, sending bolts of fire slicing down my left side. I freeze in place and try to suck in a careful breath. The pressure behind my eyes has them dragging shut, so I know this time I messed up big time.

When they reopen, the music is gone and my helmet has disappeared. Through a thick fog, I notice the smashed guardrail, red and blue lights glancing off the metal. I try to get up, but there's a crushing weight holding me down against the ground.

Heavy boots crunch against the rocky pavement and broken glass. "Are you ever gonna learn your lesson?" He lets out a long sigh. "Seriously, Lee? You really did it up this time. What were you thinking?"

"I think I need another drink. You see my bottle of Jack anywhere, Officer Declan?" If I'm hurting this bad, then I'm not drunk enough. I lick my parched lips and try again to sit up, but my left side ain't cooperating. "I'm mighty thirsty, man."

"See here, Lee, I'm gonna let the ambulance take you to the hospital, but before that happens… you have the right to remain silent. Anything you say can and will be used against you in a court of law. You have the right to an attorney. If you cannot afford an attorney— "

I manage a snort, because we both know I have more money than this entire backwater county. Something tells me I'm not going to be allowed to buy my way out of the mess I made this time. Even though I was raised in this Tennessee town and have added greatly to the local revenue since relocating my business here from California four years ago, they've not shared any of their southern hospitality with me.

Declan glares at me from underneath his hat, fat drops of rain dotting the wide brim. "…one will be appointed for you."

Two EMTs start strapping a neck brace on me and lifting whatever is left of my body onto a stretcher, and I catch a glimpse of the mangled remains of my bike dangling several yards down on the side of the guardrail.

Man… That's not going to be an easy fix.

I stifle a grunt as they lift me, thinking I'm not going to be an easy fix either.

****

After four days of staring at beige walls and medical equipment, this shake-up of scenery should be a nice change, but it isn't. Not even a little. Surrounded by dark wood walls, wood tables and chairs, I can't help but wonder why courtrooms are always dressed in so much wood…

"You may be seated," the bailiff states. The occupants of the packed-out room sit all at once like a bunch of puppets strung together.

I don't look back to acknowledge all the nosey snoops sitting behind me and keep a blank stare in place, swearing I'll give them no more fuel to add to the tabloid gossip's fire. Let it get out that a celebrity has screwed up and the public flocks to the scene like it's a spectator sport.

Celebrity. Why I've gotten grouped in the category of celebrity is beyond me. I hate that word. It sounds too close to pampered debutante to me. I've worked too hard for everything and more than earned my way. There's been nothing pampered about it.

Lance nudges my knee and draws my attention to the judge, perched on his law throne like he's king of this mountain town. Bushy eyebrows push past the edge of his bifocals, and unkempt white hair makes him appear to be old as Methuselah. The dude's façade alone could demand the room's respect if it weren't for the green chunk of broccoli wedged between his front teeth.

I'm a detail expert. Some call it a gift. At times, I call it a curse. It's a talent that makes bank when I create a new motorcycle, but it can be daunting as well. I notice everything, like the bailiff's tie is crooked. The court reporter's left earring is caught in her curly blonde hair. Both imperfections make my skin itch from needing to correct them. Or maybe the itch is the aftereffect of the wreck. Or the need for a drink.

"Son, did you hear me?"

I look back toward Judge Pruitt. "Sir?"

"I asked if you're mended enough to be here today?" Those bushy eyebrows rise over his glasses.

I think about it for a moment, not sure which is more irritating—this stranger calling me son or my bruised left side and broken arm. I try to ignore the irritation, along with the constant burn in my right palm. I rub it down the side of the coarse trousers my assistant dropped off at the hospital for this court appearance. I told the dude to bring the Tom Ford suit, but Lance advised him to bring a cheaper one. Whatever. It doesn't matter how I'm dressed, everyone in this room knows the empire I've built with my own two hands affords me only the top quality of everything. Forbes Magazine even thought it was their right to share the bottom line of my net worth, going as far as putting the eight figures in bold print.

"Mr. Sutton?"

Clearing my throat, I lie, "Yes, sir." The aches and bruises and constant dull pounding at my temples call me out on the lie, but the blank stare stays in place. It's been four days since the crash. The longest stretch of time without a drink in years. Keeping myself in check is a painful struggle.

"Good to hear." Judge Pruitt shuffles through a thick stack of papers. One of the sheets is bent, and it annoys me that he doesn't take the time to smooth it. "Let's address these charges." He goes over the DUI and other charges my aching brain doesn't take in, then gives the floor over to Lance.

"Your Honor, I've spoken with my client. Mr. Sutton knows the severity of his recklessness and is willing to do outpatient care rehab as well as paying a hefty fine."

I cut my eyes at Lance, knowing I pay him too much for that joke of an offer. Before the judge opens his mouth, I know that scenario's not happening. The old man snorts and I don't even blame him.

"This is Mr. Sutton's second DUI, and there are also a slew of misdemeanors." Judge Pruitt lifts the thick folder. The file should be cringe-worthy, but the ink stains on the side of his hand bother me more.

It might be the gnawing pain taking over my body or the all-consuming need for a drink, but I'm close to begging them to put my sorry behind in a prison cell already. Or any scenario that lets me close my eyes to this situation.

The judge sets the folder down with a hefty thump. "We have an interesting situation here. I had a private meeting this morning with a close friend about you and we both agree jail time won't do you any good, Mr. Sutton. You're too sharp for a stint in rehab, and a fine won't teach you anything."

"I completely agree, your Honor," Lance pipes in. Some of the tension relaxes in my shoulders.

"So, after much consideration, you'll be sentenced to ten months house arrest and 1,200 community service hours."

I relax a little more. There's a garage behind my place. It's equipped just as nicely as my facility in town. And I'm used to having my hands dirty, so community service won't be bothersome.

"You'll be released into the custody of Pastor Chase McCoy and will spend your ten months in an apartment behind Valley Church."

The blank stare I've been holding onto like a lifeline flounders as I backhand Lance's upper arm.

"Your Honor, a church? Surely you're not serious." Lance keeps his voice in a respectable tone, so I fight the urge to scream that the whole lot of them have lost their ever-loving minds.

"Dead serious." Judge Pruitt locks eyes with me.

"This can't be legal," Lance tries again, while I'm realizing it's time to find a new lawyer. He's worthless.

"I assure you it is." The judge glares at me, earning my glare in return. "It's only by the grace of God you're not dead, Mr. Sutton. Or even worse, you could have killed someone else with your recklessness." He has enough nerve to point an arthritic finger at me. "This is your second and final chance to get your act together."

Lance must sense I'm about to lose it, because he places a hand on my forearm. "Can't we discuss this?"

The judge shakes his head, firm with no give. "We've already discussed this a few prior times. Talking isn't getting through to your client." Pruitt turns his beady eyes back to me. "Your community service hours will be served out at the church at the pastor and his assistant's discretion. Whatever they request you do, you do it."

"So that includes animal sacrifices and other stupid religious rituals?" I rub my burning palm down the side of these uncomfortable pants. "Ain't that against my rights?" Why hasn't my stupid lawyer thought of that?

He straightens his crooked posture. "Don't get smart with me, son. I've already discussed this with Pastor McCoy. He understands that you're not required to attend services, but you will perform any task he needs done."

"What's that sh…?" I rethink my choice of words, thinking Lance should be paying me. "What's that even mean?"

"I've reviewed the list and nothing on it is against your rights. Basically, you will work off your service hours doing maintenance work. Any more questions?" Judge Pruitt directs that last bit to my incompetent lawyer.

A handyman? It's the most bogus sentence I've ever heard. "Who helped to decide all this crap?"

"We have a mutual friend who is concerned about your wellbeing." He points somewhere just behind me. "A hero in my book and I take her opinion seriously. You, son, owe her a thank you."

I glance over my shoulder just long enough to catch a glimpse of wild, light-brown hair. Neena Cameron or whatever her last name is now that's she gone and gotten married. Disgusted, I turn back to the judge. "And what if I refuse?"

Pruitt huffs and pins me with a look of pure disdain, showing we feel the same way about this mess. "Then I'd say you're a fool and will sentence you to jail."

I nod. "Ok—"

The judge holds his hand up. "You better think that through first."

Lance nudges me and whispers for me to shut up. "Your Honor, house arrest means my client would still be allowed to manage his company? Meaning business meetings on the church premises, phone and computer access, and he'll be allowed to work on projects?"

"Yes to all of that. Just as long as Mr. Sutton stays on the church property."

The judge wraps things up, but I tune him out, my mind already turning over ideas on how to get some work done from the confines of the church property. I have a crew who handles most of the bike builds and remodels, and another team of sales reps and all that, but I'm a hands-on boss and have already been out of commission for the better part of a week.

As we shuffle out of the courtroom, I give Neena a nasty look, one that I know has made grown men cower. But Neena is tougher than anyone I've ever met. She, in return, gives me a silly grin like we just won the freaking lottery with this sentence. I pass her and notice the man with thinning red hair sitting beside her. I've only attended one service at Valley Church, but the knot that man and his words from the pulpit wove in my chest that day won't let me forget him. Chase McCoy, my guardian for the next ten long months. He offers a kind smile, one I know I don't deserve. It's not a secret that I'm a certifiable jerk. Just like that, my chest is burning right along with the other aches in my body. Who is this punk? Some supernatural being?

I glare at him, too, for good measure, and follow my sorry lawyer out the door. Within an hour, my parole officer places an ankle monitor on my right leg and gives instructions on how the device works. It's clunky, and I already hate it.

Officer Abrams offers a deep scowl along with his threat. "If that little light flashes red from you wandering out of the property limits, you can guarantee I'll be on my way within seconds to cart your sorry tail off to jail. And I promise it'll be a lot longer than ten months."

He gets the blank stare, not even worth an ounce of my emotions. When I remain mute, he releases me into Chase McCoy's custody.

"Is this really happening?" I ask Lance in the hall. He promises to get to work on an appeal. He'd better.

The sunshades Lance hands me just before we breach the doorway of the courthouse help to hide my wince as I take in the sight before me. Every inch of me hurts like a toothache, and the burning in my palm is reaching an entirely new level of torture. Cameras flash and questions are yelled in my direction from rubberneckers showing up to witness my walk of shame, but I'm a pro at ignoring them and handle it like a boss until I'm tucked inside McCoy's beat-up station wagon. To make matters worse, it's foreign.

He slowly drives us out of the chaos and down the road splitting the town between the mountain valleys. Sweat is running down the back of my collar and my mouth is like cotton, both of which are making it impossible to ignore the pounding headache.

"Neena said she has a meeting, but she'll be by to check on you in a day or two."

I manage to find the lever and shove the seat back so my legs aren't so cramped. "You might want to tell her to leave me the…" I catch the swear before it slips out. Proof, that even though I'm reeling in pain, I do know how to use some manners. "Just tell her it's best she leaves me alone for a while."

The pastor turns on his blinker light and makes a right. There's a slight whine in the steering, but it's doubtful he even notices. Of course, I notice and now the itch to fix it is driving me nuts. I take a breath and rub my temples.

"Surely you're grateful Neena got you out of going to jail?"

"Jail. Church. Same difference." I shrug my right shoulder, the one not beat and bruised and stitched, but I doubt he sees. He doesn't even acknowledge my comment.

"You must be famished. I can swing in somewhere. Whatcha in the mood for?" Pastor Chase seems to sense my headache situation and turns the radio off.

"An ice-cold beer to start." I can barely swallow with the need for it.

He laughs like I made joke. "Any fast food place? Tacos? Burgers? A bucket of chicken?"

"Whatever is fine. Don't care," I mutter, resting my head against the passenger window.

Tasteless burgers ain't fine, but that's what I get for saying whatever. We arrive at the red-brick church within minutes of choking down the joke of a meal, still slurping on the syrupy sweet soda. He drives around back and parks at a two-story garage dressed in cheap white siding. The windows are planked by just-as-cheap black shutters. The opposite of my sprawling nothing-cheap-about-it log cabin.

"This will be home for the next ten months. My assistant has done a nice job of fixing up the apartment over the garage. The church uses it as a guesthouse for visiting speakers and such, but…"

The pastor grabs a duffle bag out of his trunk, the same bag the guard confiscated when I had it dropped off at the hospital. He leads the way up a narrow set of steps inside the cluttered garage. If I'm stuck here for the unforeseeable future, that's the first thing that needs to be fixed. I don't do clutter and disorder.

"I'm allowed to use this space, Pastor?"

He glances over his shoulder, eyeing the lopsided mountain of boxes, scattered Christmas decorations, and other junk. "Just call me Chase, and yes. You're welcome to use the space." He opens the door to the top floor.

Lemony furniture polish and some kind of fake floral scent hit me first, followed by the sight of the bland room. I scan the wood-panel walls until landing on the scented plugin that's responsible for kicking this nasty headache up several notches. I yank the stinking thing out of the plug and hand it over to Chase.

He eyes it before cramming it into his pocket. "I'll let you settle in today and we'll go over your duties tomorrow. The first few weeks will be light tasks, so you can heal. The doctor went over your injuries with me earlier. Broken arm, two cracked ribs, and a deeply bruised hip. Some stitches on your shoulder. He said it would be helpful in your healing if you remain active, but please let me know if something is too much."

I refrain from snorting, surprised Dr. Henson didn't order me to start chopping wood and walk-mowing acres of land. It's no secret that one of my misdemeanor charges includes the good ole doc, sometime after he caught his wife behind the desk in my office, doing a little more than just writing a check for his custom bike. How he was allowed to treat me is beyond my understanding, and I suspect Henson is the reason I didn't get any decent pain meds.

"I'm allowed to get someone to bring me more clothes and necessities, right?" I ask, looking through the meager bag. I grab the bottle of Ibuprofen from underneath a stack of T-shirts and wash three pills down with what's left of the soda. I toss the empty cup into a trashcan near the window unit and take a second to fiddle with the dial to set it to a cooler temperature.

"Yes... Just no alcohol and drugs. Oh, and no overnight guests." The guy gives me a look that clears up what he means by *guests*. No *women*.

"Gotcha, man." I eye the full-sized bed, knowing it won't accommodate my 6'3" frame. "How about furniture? Am I allowed to bring some in?" I motion toward the tiny bed with my casted arm, trying to twist my wrist slightly to ease some of the itch concealed underneath.

"I don't suppose that's against the rules." Chase points out the dorm-sized fridge and microwave, both a joke. "My assistant is out shopping for some food supplies. She should be by in just a little while. Do you need anything until then?"

"Nah." I pull my phone and the charger out and plug it up behind the small corner table. With its two plastic chairs, the set looks more fitting for a patio. This place certainly ain't for long stays, but there are no water leaks on the ceiling. No rat traps in the corners. It gives off a nice enough vibe, but also whispers for you not to linger too long. Ten minutes is too long, let alone ten months.

Chase goes over a few more things before leaving me to it. I sit at the small table and inspect the black contraption around my ankle. It's bulky and no way will my regular motorcycle boots work with it. I pick up the phone and fire off a list of things needed to my assistant.

Yo. Need low-rise boots. Size 12. If not, black Chucks will do. King-sized bedframe and extra soft mattress set.

Sheets and all that too. Black-out curtains. My laptop. An updated bike build schedule. And a flat-screen smart TV. ASAP.

Drew texts back—*On it, boss.*

He better be on it for what I pay him. I text—*You have two hours to make it happen.*

Drew sends a thumbs-up, and he's true to his word. Within two hours he's hanging up my new curtains as I sit on the end of the bed eating a proper meat-and-potatoes meal from the best restaurant in town, Charlie Mike. The bed takes up almost the entire room and makes for a tight walk to get to the small bathroom on the right of it, but who cares.

"Anything else?" Drew twirls the screwdriver in the air before tucking it into his back pocket. He pulls out a sour apple Dum Dum sucker, unwraps it, and pops it in his mouth. He's only twenty-two but has managed to grow a long enough beard he could pass as a ZZ Top offspring.

"I'm good for now. You're free to go." I hand him the empty plate and the punk has enough nerve to laugh.

"Yeah, that only makes one of us." Drew's laughter cuts off when he notices I don't find the stupid joke amusing in the least. He's quick to dash out the door.

I'm about to lie back and try to forget this day when a dark-haired angel with legs for miles walks in.

"Sweet. I thought my assistant forgot dessert." I lick my lips and ease to my feet, trying to cover up the fact that my entire body is screaming in pain. I'm still wearing the cheap navy suit, but I've lost the tie and unfastened several of the shirt buttons. Call it vain, but I know even in this beaten state I still look good. From the way this babe is taking me in, she agrees.

"I'm just—"

"Just too fine for words."

This gorgeous woman is a cross between Pocahontas and an Amazonian princess. Tall and sturdy, and suddenly my new favorite fantasy. She makes her plain outfit of jeans and a top look anything but plain.

She points over my shoulder and takes a step out of reach. "Where's the other bed?"

"Mine ate it for a snack. This one's memory foam. Top quality. You wanna take off your clothes and test it out with me?"

Her golden eyes widen. Man, those jewels are wicked. I'm talking liquid gold.

"What? No!" She waves her hand in the air. "How dare you talk to a woman wearing a wedding ring like that!"

I don't bother to look at the ring, knowing the piece of jewelry is meaningless. "Sweetheart, your husband obviously ain't taking care of you if you're up here in my room panting like this." I motion toward her rapidly rising chest and the next thing I know the left side of my face is on fire.

Even though being slapped is enough to make me cuss, I hold it in and yell, "I think I'm in love," hoping she hears me as she stomps down the stairs. I want her to storm back in here and spar with me, but the side door slams on that idea.

I notice several bags of groceries by the door and almost feel bad for how I treated her. It looks like she may be the maid or something, and it's never wise to tick off the help.

Chapter Two

Bellamy

Livid and fuming, I don't bother knocking before marching into Chase's office. "Tell me you didn't do what I think you did!"

Chase looks up from a stack of papers on his desk and takes off his readers. "Huh?"

"Don't play dumb, Chase! You told me we had a guest. Not a criminal!"

"Calm down, Bellamy." He motions to the chair, but I remain standing. "Did something happen?"

"He made a pass at me." I begin to pace around the office, recalling that devil-may-care grin on the man's face just before I slapped it off.

Chase goes to stand. "I'll have a talk—"

"No, I already took care of it." I wave for him to sit back down.

Chase stands anyway, preparing to leave. "Did he touch you?"

"No. Nothing like that. He was just running off at the mouth." I motion for him to sit again and this time he listens. My red palm catches my attention, reminding me I was the one who did the touching. Can't believe I just slapped someone for the very first time. Ever. Not sure if that's something to be proud of or not.

"Listen, Bellamy—"

"Lee Sutton? Really, Chase?" There's no way anyone can live in Clarks, Tennessee and not know who the infamous bad boy is, and the fact that he is a womanizing, arrogant jerk. Images of the tattooed, blond menace to society are constantly popping up on newsfeeds like there's nothing important to report on around here other than his philandering escapades that normally land him in the back of a cop car.

"I'm still going to have a talk with him, but we need to have a talk first. Now sit down."

I plop down in a chair across from Chase and cross my arms. We've worked together here at the church for five years, but I've known him since I was only eighteen and in love with his younger brother. Thirteen years total, yet this is the first time in the history of our relationship that my brother-in-law has royally ticked me off.

After he gives me the rundown that now has me mad at my friend Neena as well, Chase hands over a list of Lee's duties.

"He should probably still be in the hospital if you ask me, so we'll just let him lay low a few more days to recuperate. After that, he can start on the lighter tasks, like trash pickup and weeding flowerbeds."

I skim the list and come to a halt on item fourteen. "You've assigned him to take up the offering on Sunday mornings?"

"Yes, it's the only way I can get him into service without it being against his rights." Chase answers an email as I sit here staring him down.

"Chase," I say sternly enough to get his attention. "This is something the church members may not take too kindly to. You're asking for it."

He hits a key on the computer and turns his undivided attention toward me. "If a member has a problem with it, I'll be sure to tell them what I'm about to tell you. My brother's entire life was devoted to evangelism. Beau went on his first mission trip when he was two years old." Chase takes a steady breath and continues in a much quieter tone. "I know it's not easy for you to hear, but he would have wanted you to reach those who needed Jesus, and that includes a man with a DUI."

I lean back in the chair. I'm not sure if Chase is referring to Lee Sutton or Carl Waverly, who's serving a life sentence for taking my husband's life.

"I'm not the right person to help you with this." I place the list on his cluttered desk.

"No, Bellamy. I think you're the perfect person. Two years... It's time to come to terms with it. To move on. If we both can help rehabilitate someone like Sutton, then maybe we can forgive Waverly and find some closure."

I'm pretty sure Chase has already forgiven the man who took Beau's life, but that sharp sting hasn't ebbed for me since that awful night. "You're wrong. I'm still too broken. Hurt and resentment are still pouring out of my wounds."

"I'm in town for the next several days straight before I have to head out to that conference in Atlanta. Let me take care of things with Sutton while you pray about it. If you still don't feel up to the task, then I'll find someone else."

I nod and go to stand, hating that this should be easier to agree on. No matter how much I want to deny it, Beau would be the first in line to help someone get their life sorted, Carl Waverly included. But I'm not my extraordinary husband. I'm a bitter widow.

I slip out of the office and walk the quiet hall to the side entrance. The parking lot is already filling up and the day is turning to dusk. It's almost time for the Wednesday night service to begin, but I'm in no mood to be around anyone, so I load up in my truck and drive the short distance to my apartment.

The first task after making it inside is to switch on all the lights even though there's not many in this tiny one-bedroom bungalow I moved into after Beau's death. It was too difficult to continue living in our house where we filled it with love and dreams. It all died right along with Beau.

I brought home some unwanted guests from the morgue that night. Erratic sleep patterns, memories of his lifeless body slicing through the darkness to attack me, and a debilitating loneliness are the worst of them. When Carl Waverly chose to get behind the wheel of his car after consuming his weight in alcohol, he changed the entire trajectory of my life. Instead of making babies and memories with my husband, I'm left afraid of the dark with a dismal sense of being absolutely abandoned.

I grab the quilt off the back of the couch and burrow underneath it while turning on the TV and hitting the play button. The void of the room comes to life from the deep boom of Beau's laughter. His cheeks are high in color and those green eyes just sparkle with happiness as he drinks punch from a pineapple. It's probably standard widow protocol to watch the wedding video, but I've attached myself to the video of Beau's thirtieth birthday party. Less than a month before he would be taken from me way too soon.

Taking a deep breath, my attention latches on to the lively party. It was filmed in our old backyard with Beau surrounded by his youth group. Everyone is vibrant in colorful Hawaiian patterned shirts and plastic leis. Beau sets the silly drink down and has just agreed to an eating contest with several teenage boys. They demolish dozens of brightly colored cupcakes right before my eyes. Beau has orange icing smeared on his cheek and is laughing too hard to eat anymore. The man would have made the best daddy.

It's thirty-seven minutes of jubilant laughter where my husband is kept front and center. A happy version of me is close to his side in most of those minutes, but my eyes stay trained on Beau until his laughing stops and the screen goes blank.

I ran out of tears sometime last year. Like one day, the well finally dried up. Before that, this is where I'd curl into a ball and sob. Now, I just restart the video and stare motionless at my sweet husband until sleep shows up for a short spell.

****

Over a week has passed by with no Lee Sutton in sight. If Chase has him doing anything to start working off the community service, he's kept quiet about it. But today that all ends, because my brother-in-law had to go out of town and left me as the warden.

Before I even make it to my parking spot at the back of the church, something out of the ordinary catches my attention. Two beefy motorcycles are parked by the garage. Looking around, I spot two burly guys walking around with garbage bags.

I hurry out of the truck and walk toward them. "Excuse me, gentlemen. What are y'all doing?"

The lanky one with an impressively long, white beard holds up the trash bag with a *duh* expression. I'm talking snow-white. Even in this July heat his head is covered with a black beanie, but the edges give way to the matching snow-white hair underneath. Bet he spends a good bit of time at the salon to keep his roots in check.

"Yes, but why are you two picking up trash?" I wrack my brain, trying to remember if we had others assigned to community service. It's not uncommon, but I'm too on top of the schedule for this to have slipped my mind.

The dark-skinned guy with dreadlocks drops the bag and walks over, seeming more social than the other guy who keeps picking up trash like a robot. "Yo, I'm Ace." He holds his gloved hand out but then thinks better of it and drops it to his side.

"Bellamy." I smile even though it doesn't go anywhere close to my eyes.

Ace hitches a thumb toward the other guy. "That's Drew. We're here to help Lee out. He ain't feeling the best."

I blink at Ace then look over at Drew, who's peeping over his shoulder at me while rolling a sucker around his mouth. "I'm sorry, but this is not how community service works. Lee has to do the work."

Ace raises his palms. "But he's the boss and—"

"He's not the boss here. Sorry, but I'm going to have to ask you two to leave." I point over to their bikes to make myself clear.

"Man…" Drew walks both fairly-empty trash bags over to the dumpster beside the garage. He mutters what sounds like a swear word under his breath. "She's gonna get us in trouble."

They legitimately sound worried, but there's no way Lee is going to be allowed to sling his clout around here like I'm sure he's used to doing. After the two guys finally load up on their bikes and, in a mean roar, peel out of the church parking lot, I head upstairs to see who Lee Sutton thinks he is. King he is not, and it's time he comes to an understanding about how things are going to work around here.

I have enough wits about me to knock this time.

"Come in," Lee's raspy voice calls out.

"It's Bellamy," I announce while letting myself in, but come to an automatic halt. "Do you have clothes on underneath that blanket?" His top half is bare, showing off a museum's worth of art decorating his skin, so I have my doubts.

Lee rolls to his back, hissing in the process, and lifts his heavy eyelids. His blue eyes are glassy and he looks a little disoriented. He fists the edge of the blanket, preparing to sling it off.

"Don't you dare lift that!" I take a step back, preparing to flee.

"Then don't ask stupid questions." Lee slowly sits up, his movements quite stiff. "Look, sweetheart, I'll let you take a look. All's you gotta do is ask nicely."

"That's it!" I yank my phone out of my pocket. "I'm calling Judge Pruitt."

Lee pushes the blanket off to show that he's wearing pajama pants before swinging his feet off the side of the bed. His left side faces me and I'm shocked at what's exposed.

"Oh my... That's rather colorful."

Lee looks up and sways slightly. "You into ink, babe?"

"My name is Bellamy. Not babe, or sweetheart, or whatever else you think sounds cute." I have nothing against tattoos, but I won't be sharing that with him. I wave a hand toward his side. "And I'm talking about the bruising and scrapes." The edges are fading to a yellowish green, but there's more deep purple and red than evidence of it healing. The parts that aren't bruised look raw, like something tried taking his skin off.

He glances at his side before rolling his eyes. "Oh, that's just where the guardrail broke my fall."

I ignore his grouchy tone and ask in a softer tone, "Are you okay?"

"I'm not sure, but I think I have a fever and my hand is killing me." He opens his right hand and shows me the angry redness of his rather puffy palm.

"That doesn't look so good." I know I need to straighten him out about the community service deal and how he can't make his minions do the work for him, but at the moment his health overrules the lecture. "What's your doctor's name?"

"He ain't a fan of mine so don't bother." Lee makes a move to run his hand through his disheveled blond hair but drops the swollen hand at the last minute, then tries with the casted hand and gets frustrated to the point that a litany of explicit words breaks free from his chapped lips. His fingers are free from the cast but it still seems too daunting.

I steel myself and brave placing my palm against his forehead. He's scorching hot to the touch and is swaying. Worrying the fever has him dehydrated, I grab a bottle of water from the fridge and coerce him into drinking it. "Lee, I'm going to call my friend who's a Nurse Practitioner to come over and check on you. Lie back down for now."

He grumbles some incoherent nonsense, but falls back onto his pillows while I pull my phone out and dial Mia's number.

Four rings in, I'm about to hang up and call 911 but relief washes over me when Mia finally answers. I explain the symptoms and who is in need, and Mia agrees with a great deal of reluctance to come over and check on Lee. I'm not sure if she despises him on principle as I do or if there's something else. Either way, the man needs medical care, something he obviously didn't properly receive while he was in the hospital.

I sit in a chair by the bed, watching Lee shiver even though his bare torso glistens with a sheen of perspiration, mad at myself for caring so much about this criminal's wellbeing. This is already too complicated and it's just getting started.

Chapter Three

Lee

One time, when I was probably close to eight years old, my old man took me and Tommy to the river. Sun up to sundown, we fished and picnicked and frolicked in the water. It was a blast. Maybe even the best day of my life. Or it was until later that night when I woke up feeling like my skin was on fire. Turns out that much exposure without sunblock can lead to a nasty case of sun poisoning. On top of that, I managed to get eaten up by redbugs. It was singularly the most miserable night of my life.

Sun poisoning and redbugs don't even come close to the hell I'm trapped in at the moment. "I think I'm dying…" Head pounding and body screaming in some evil chilly heat. "Just saw my hand off." I hold it over to Mia Calder, thinking she's probably just a hallucination.

I tried talking her into playing nurse with me a few years ago, but she was too decent to agree. She's definitely in a category of her own, and here she is looking down at my hand with concern pinching her beautiful face.

Yeah, I'm hallucinating. Wanting to just go back to sleep, I drop my hand and go to roll over but she grabs ahold of my wrist before I can.

"Oh sugar… Be still and let me get a good look at it." Mia pulls my hand closer as she sits on the edge of the bed.

"The husband alright with you being here?"

"The husband drove me and is now sitting outside the door on the stairs, so yes." She smooths her fingertip over a tender spot, making me flinch.

"It feels like there are a million splinters in there, or ants, but I can't see anything."

"It's probably closer to road debris." She lets go of my hand and checks my side and then the stitches on the back of my shoulder. "What medications did they send home with you?"

"Ibuprofen." I lean back on the pile of pillows after Mia finishes examining me. The pain slicing through me won't even let me enjoy her hands on my body.

"Seriously?"

"Yeah. Henson ain't a fan."

Understanding dawns on her pretty face, so I'm guessing she saw that particular headline from last spring. "No matter, Henson took an oath and he broke it by not providing you with proper treatment." Mia shakes her head and calls out for the husband.

"Yes, ma'am?" Bode asks Mia as he cuts his eyes at me with as much love as a rabid Rottweiler. If I felt better I'd give it right back to him.

"I need you to go to the pharmacy. I'll have a list texted to your phone by the time you get there. And I'm calling in two prescriptions that'll need to be picked up."

"Nah, Mia. I'll call my assistant to go." I reach for my phone on the nightstand, but end up knocking it to the floor.

"Bode doesn't mind." Mia turns her attention to the husband where he looks like he does mind. A lot.

Huffing, Bode stalks over and kisses her, marking his territory. "Lee, you want some breakfast while I'm out?" Bode asks, shocking me.

"That's a great idea, honey," Mia pipes in.

"Nah—"

"I'm calling you in a pain med and an antibiotic, so you'll need to eat before taking either."

Pain meds sound like a dream, so I don't argue with her. "My wallet is on that table," I tell Bode, but he ignores me and heads out. I'm all out confused that either one of them would be so kind to me after I tried unraveling their marriage. "I deserve for you to treat me like Henson treated me."

Mia goes over to the small fridge and comes back with a bottle of water. "Good thing God doesn't treat us how we deserve to be treated. He's who I model my life after." She uncaps the bottle and hands it to me. "Honestly, Lee, you should have died in that wreck."

"Wow, sweetheart. Tell me how you really feel." I don't even want to drink the water now, but she points at the bottle with a stern glare, so I take a sip.

"You know what I mean. Even with a helmet on, you shouldn't have been able to walk away from it. God is giving you another shot at this life. You serving house arrest here is a divine appointment."

I snort. "Ain't nothing divine about it."

"I beg to differ. Neena told me what strings she pulled to get you here. The least you can do is try to make the best of it."

"Your sister needs to learn to mind her own business."

"Yeah. I'm not sure she thought this one through." Mia shoots a look out the door and then sits back on the side of the bed. "Can I ask you a favor?"

"Babe, I'm not up for much, but—"

"Seriously, Lee." Mia glares, looking offended, instantly making me feel bad that I couldn't keep my mouth closed for once. "Please don't give Bellamy a hard time."

"Then she shouldn't be such a pill." I hand Mia the bottle. "That babe needs to loosen up and spend more *quality* time with her husband." I try to waggle my eyebrows, but that even hurts to do.

Mia sucks her teeth and leers closer. "Her husband is dead." She lets that sink in before adding, "Beau was killed by a *drunk* driver."

I vaguely remember slinging off about the woman's husband the other day after she tried shoving her wedding ring in my face. The water starts trying to climb back up my throat, making it difficult to swallow. Swearing under my breath, I look anywhere but at Mia. "This is jacked up."

Mia shuts up after this, and I grow mute too.

Once Bode gets back with the supplies, Mia sets up some kind of soak for my hand and then cleans and redresses my side and shoulder. That's all fine and dandy until she dries my hand off and begins stabbing at it with tweezers. Like a magician, Mia starts producing little slivers of glass, rock, and other junk out of my palm. It hurts like a mother, but after another soaking, some food, and then the meds, the pain is receding for the first time since the accident and my eyelids won't stay open.

****

Misery must certainly love company, because for the last few days this broad keeps showing up uninvited, putting up with my lip while making sure I take the meds Mia prescribed and feeding me. I ain't made it easy on her, but she knows how to hold her own. Standing before me now with her hands on her slender hips, golden eyes molten, she's preparing for another round.

I hold up the fistful of bedding. "It's just sheets. What's got you in such a tizzy over sheets?"

"Doing your laundry is not a part of my job. I'm the church secretary and Chase's assistant. Not your maid." Bellamy smooths a hand down the side of her dressy trousers—to make a point, perhaps. Her black hair is pinned back in a severe bun, and a simple blouse and boring heels add to the fantasy of naughty librarian. The only thing missing is a sassy pair of glasses.

I toss the sheets back onto the floor and kick them out of the way while making a mental note to get Drew on buying some new ones. Mia showed up here last night with a shot of high-test antibiotic after the pills didn't seem to be doing the trick. The fever finally disappeared sometime before dawn, so hopefully that's the end of the sweaty chills purgatory.

"Did you hear me? I'm not your—"

"Then stop acting like one." I point to the plate of food on the table. It looks like a fat fried pork chop and mashed potatoes. She brings food, attitude, and a list of chores each day. And each day, we go a round or two about something.

"It's called being polite, you hateful jerk."

"Call it what you want. I still didn't ask for it." I turn my back to Bellamy, wanting her gone, and skim over today's handyman duties. "How am I supposed to blow the freaking parking lot with cracked ribs?" I glance over my shoulder and see her snatching the steaming plate up and heading to the door. "You might as well leave it, since you went through the trouble of bringing it up here."

"I have a good mind to smash it into your face, but I think I'll just give it to the stray cat outside so it won't go to waste. I'm sure he has enough decency not to turn up his nose at home cooking. And it's not a backpack blower. It's one of those you walk behind. Nothing wrong with your legs."

The door slams, leaving behind the savory scent of me blowing my meal ticket. I give her a few minutes to ride her broom to wherever before heading down and out the side door of the garage. Slurping sounds draw my attention to the ground where a mangy looking creature is devouring my lunch.

I've seen dogs without tails, but never a cat without one. Until now. It's a dark-gray, fluffy thing that should be lounging on a pillow in a posh cat food commercial, if it weren't for not having a tail. Plus, there's a fairly large patch of fur missing on its right hip.

"Looks like life ain't treating you any better than it's treating me," I tell it, but the cat's too engrossed with the pork chop. "Enjoy."

I leave the scraggly animal to its feast and go over to the shed to unearth the blower. It's front and center, so not much effort is taken to find it, but the pull cord indicates it's going to take much more effort to crank the ancient machine. After checking and finding the fuel tank full, I pull it out and brace myself while gripping the cord. With my casted arm tucked close to my bruised ribs to protect them, I yank the cord with it only producing a cough. After a few more tries, my side is throbbing and the thing is still dead.

"You're too spoiled to even handle this without an assistant?" Bellamy says, coming from out of nowhere. She drops a purse and a stack of folders to the ground. I get a whiff of her as she nudges me out of the way.

Most women smell as fake as they act, like super-sweet flowers or fruit. But Bellamy carries a spicy scent, giving off the impression she spends her days baking spiced muffins instead of stomping around this old church building. It's a warm, inviting scent, and I like it even though I hate liking it.

Without a word, she adjusts the throttle, fiddles with the choke, and then yanks the cord with precision. It comes to life on her first try. With a sardonic flourish of her hand, she presents it to me, picks up her stuff, and walks over to a dually truck.

"You're just going to leave me here all alone? It'll be mighty tempting to execute a prison break," I speak over the whine of the blower before she gets the door shut. She's tall enough that it didn't even take any effort to climb inside the giant truck.

"You're forgetting that cute anklet you're wearing?" Bellamy gives me a bored look and motions to my leg where my jeans are covering the device. "Be sure to stay within the parking and playground area or you'll be breaking out of this prison for another one." She cranks the beast, sending a deep rumble from the diesel engine and goose bumps to break out over my skin.

Dumbfounded, I watch the slick, pearl-white crew-cab roll out of the parking lot. That should not have been hot, but that gorgeous, grumpy woman showing the blower who's boss and then driving off in a killer truck... Yeah. That was hot.

And this is not going to work. I explain as much to my lawyer when he facetimes me after I finish my grunt work for the day.

"God is playing some sick joke on me," I tell Lance while trying to wedge a pen inside my cast to reach an unreachable itch.

"How?"

I give up and toss the pen across the room, then reposition the phone where I have it propped up against the lamp on the nightstand. "I'm caged in a church of all places. It's been two weeks without a drop of alcohol and no action, and I'm stuck spending my days with the woman of my dreams *and* nightmares."

Lance chuckles.

"It ain't funny. There's no way I can handle this for ten months. Man, you gotta get me out of here." I rub my palm against the coarse cast. It's a healing itch instead of the burning, but it's driving me crazy just the same.

"Let me see what I can do, but it'll probably only be a reduced sentence and that's only if you behave. So take a cold shower."

"I've been behaving. And the shower stall barely fits me." Nothing fits me here. I lean closer to the screen. "You have no idea how much torture it is having this hot woman parading around me every day."

"Is she dressing inappropriately? Hitting on you?"

Bellamy dresses too appropriately, and the only thing she's come close to hitting was me upside the head yesterday with a feather duster when I told her where she could stick it. "No. Neither." I run my fingers through my hair, knowing I'm past time for a trimming.

Lance leans back in his fancy desk chair and steeples his hands. "Maybe this'll do you good. Teach you some self-restraint, so when you do get out of there it'll be easier to stay out of trouble. Look at this as a life lesson and—"

I hit the end button, pick up the phone, and shoot him a text. *I don't pay you for pep talks. Don't bother me again until you find a way to get me out of here. Hurry!*

A few seconds pass before I remember something else he needs to do to earn his paycheck. I send another text. *And find out if it's against my rights to have to collect the offering on Sundays.*

I was informed earlier that I'd be doing that from now on, but I have no desire to step foot into that sanctuary on Sundays. One visit a year ago was enough to never want to go back.

Chapter Four

Bellamy

The tinkering sound of productivity comes from the garage as I walk into the open bay door. Surprisingly, the inside is immaculate with everything somehow finding a proper storage place. Christmas decorations are hanging from hooks on the ceiling. Dozens of plastic totes line the back wall with what I hope were the contents of the missing boxes. What's most surprising are the neatly placed food and water bowls near the door. I scan the room until finding the stray cat lounging on a new bed.

The idea of Lee taking care of a stray animal is intriguing, but I hold my tongue and move over to where he's working. Laid out on a mat is a sea of mechanical parts, meticulously lined up. Beside it is a crumpled motorcycle that Lee is working on tearing apart. I keep quiet and just watch him for a few minutes. When I picture a mechanic, I picture a burly guy smeared head-to-toe in grease and grime. Not this man. His jeans and black T-shirt are clean and he's wearing a rubber glove on his right hand. Not sure if that's his normal or if he's doing it to protect his palm.

In the short time Lee has been here, it's become clear that his wild reputation may not be entirely accurate. For such a bad boy, he's quite domestic. His room is always tidy and his bed made each morning when I go in to do the daily sweep for any contraband. The detailed list he keeps on bike builds and his other business affairs is so orderly that it's borderline OCD.

"What is all this?" I ask when he keeps on ignoring me standing right in front of him.

Lee looks up but keeps working a bolt loose. His cobalt-blue eyes are guarded as if they are holding a plethora of secrets, yet the starbursts of lighter blue near the irises seem to be on the verge of spilling each and every one of them.

Once he has the bolt in his hand, he finally answers me. "It's a stupid reminder. Time to fix it."

"Fix what? The reminder or the stupidity behind it?" The condescending remark is past my lips before I can stop it. Honestly, I don't talk to people the way I do this man, but I seem to be unable to help myself.

His eyebrows hitch up. "Both."

The overhead light catches on the dainty silver ring on his left pinky where it's peeking from the edge of his cast. I've noticed it a few times, thinking it's a bit too feminine for such an infamous bad boy.

"What's up with that ring?" I point at it.

Lee wiggles the front fender loose and places it on the mat. It's smashed beyond repair, in my opinion. "Another reminder," he mutters before going to work on the back fender.

"An ex-wife?"

Lee snorts and shakes his head. "Babe, I have better sense than to put a ring on a chick's finger." He raises his casted arm and looks at the dainty ring. "This was my mother's wedding band."

My chest squeezes. "Oh... I'm sorry. I didn't know she passed."

"She's not dead. As far as I know, she's shacking up with some bum down in Tuscaloosa."

"Oh, well... that's great—"

"Yeah. Wonderful. Ma's a peach for walking out on her family. After my little brother died, she packed her bags, handed me this little token of a broken promise, and left. Said she couldn't deal." Lee huffs and shakes his head while glaring at the ring, growing rather agitated. "Try making a ten-year-old kid understand why he ain't enough to stick around for."

Clearly, Lee has momma issues, but I think the loss of his brother is where most of his hurt lies. It was easy to catch the slight cringe when he mentioned his brother. It's the same reaction I have when I mention Beau. Death hurts no matter the age, but I'm guessing there is a unique hurt in a category entirely on its own that attaches itself to the death of a child.

I know I should leave well enough alone, but ask, "Then why wear her ring?"

The wrench clatters to the floor with intentional force before Lee picks up another tool and starts in on removing the mangled handlebars. "It's a reminder to keep women in their place. To love 'em and leave 'em."

"You don't know the first thing about love," I fire back, indignation rapidly coming to a boil. "You use them."

"You're like one of those dumb, yapping lap dogs!" The tool bounces off the wall as his rugged face grows red. "You don't know when to shut up. Yap, yap, yap!" Lee turns and walks over to a massive toolbox, releasing a steady stream of curse words at a quicker pace than him walking away. Even with a slight limp, he has quite a self-assured swagger. A walk all his own—confident with a heaping amount of attitude.

I hate his walk and everything he represents. The man is the very definition of everything I find repulsive. Selfish and dangerous, not caring who he hurts with his careless behavior. It's like being stuck with a burlier version of Carl Waverly.

I take a step back and watch him pick up a tool, throw a tool, and repeat—all the while muttering bitter words peppered with obscenities.

"Three weeks in this hole!" He tosses something else with it pinging off the workbench. "Need a drink... Coming out of my skin... Feel like a caged animal..."

My grandma used to warn that there was a time to remain quiet and let hurt run its course. Watching Lee come unglued, it's clearly one of those times. Cautiously, I take another step back as he keeps unraveling. A tear slips out the corner of his eye and shocks me.

"Lee?"

He turns his back completely and bats the tear away while shaking his head in warning.

I've never met such an undeserving man in my entire life, yet I still silently call out to God to help him. As I pray, a phantom reaction to wrap my arms around Lee and offer comfort slams into me from out of nowhere. It's unnerving to the point of sending me scurrying out of the garage.

Before I shut the side door, I remember the purpose of me coming here in the first place. I'm about to just leave him alone for the time being when I hear Lee call me a choice word, and all the empathy I was feeling for the hateful man evaporates. "Go ahead and have yourself a temper tantrum, but once you get it out, the church needs pressure washing." I rush out the door when I hear another tool making contact with the wall.

My office window gives an unobstructed view of the left side of the church, so for most of the day I get a front-row seat to Lee wrestling with the pressure washer while blessing it out, even kicking it a few times. The man is mad at the world today, and I'm a little ashamed of myself for poking the bear earlier. Good thing the children's Bible school program has wrapped for the summer with school getting back into session in another week. He's in no shape to be around anyone, least of all children.

Even in all his fury, Lee stops at some point to walk over and feed the stray cat, going as far as squatting down to pet it. It's strange to see him perform such a gentle act after his show of intimidating rage.

After I finish up the workday, I head outside and find Lee walking hasty circles around the parking lot, looking much like the caged animal he claims to be. I try not to, but find myself feeling sorry for him.

"Just leave me alone, Belle." Lee turns in the opposite direction to get away from me, and I'm glad because he doesn't catch me balking.

No one has ever called me Belle besides my husband. Lee is still fuming, so I doubt he even realizes he did it, but I did and have to blink back the sudden stinging in my eyes.

"I lied to you," I blurt, causing Lee to cast an incredulous look over his wide shoulder.

Lee turns around and waits for me to catch up to him. He's a considerable height and built like a tank. Even though I'm on the tall side, he is still overwhelming when I look up at him.

"Mrs. Holier than Thou lied?" His left eyebrow arches.

I hold both hands up. "Could you just *not* for a minute?"

The harshness collecting around his eyes and mouth softens a bit as he waves a hand for me to get on with it.

"Remember when we went over the limitations to the ankle monitor?"

"Yeah. The parking lot and the playground area." He points to the playset on the other side of the garage, reminding me that at some point I'm supposed to have him sand and reseal it.

"Well, last week Chase talked to the judge and had the perimeter extended to include all of the church property in case he needs you to do some other work, like pick up limbs and mow."

"So I'm allowed to walk on that track back there where you run in the mornings?"

"Yes." I'm surprised he's even seen me do that. It's close enough to my apartment that I can get in an earlier morning run and go back home to clean up before work.

He scratches at the edge of the cast near his elbow. "That's not lying if he just had it changed."

"Lie of omission." I shrug, taken aback that he's giving me an out. "Well, there's more to the property than the track and well... I thought maybe I could show you something."

Lee looks around indecisively as the breeze plays through his dark-blond locks of hair. A barber showed up yesterday to trim it, leaving the top much longer than the closely buzzed sides, styled in a rugged hipster fashion. For the first time since he arrived here his face is stubble-free and showing off the muscle ticking along his jaw, so I guess the barber gave him a shave as well.

On a long sigh, he mutters, "Sure. I guess."

I turn around and head toward the patch of woods behind the church, knowing he's following by the crunching of leaves and snapping of twigs from his heavy boots.

Lee stops a few times to make sure the monitor isn't flashing red, maybe not quite trusting me. That's okay. I don't trust him either.

We keep walking until reaching my favorite spot.

"A waterfall," Lee states.

Water rushes down the wall of rocks and hushes the world beyond the trees. It's not very large, maybe nine or ten feet tall where it spills into a shallow pool, but in my eyes, it's the picture of tranquility. "I know it's not much, but you're allowed to come back here and get away when you need to."

Lee eases his large body onto a big rock and regards the shower of water. "After the way I acted this morning, I wouldn't blame you one bit for not sharing this with me."

I think that was his way of apologizing, but I'm just as much at fault as Lee. It was me who instigated his tirade, after all.

Mesmerized by the cascading water, I choose a boulder beside his and sit down. A fine mist finds its way to me, but it's so refreshing that I decide to stay put and allow it to cool my heated face. We remain quiet as a few birds squawk from a nearby tree. The area is secluded by the shelf of rock, yet it gives off the impression of openness, so I hope he feels a little freer. Nine more months will be a painful time for the both of us, if he doesn't settle in somehow.

"I'm going to head home. I'll email you the property coordinates so you'll know the exact range, but for now just don't go any further than the waterfall and you'll be fine."

Lee only nods, his eyes still fastened to the water as he fiddles with the ring on his pinky, making it clear what his mind is focused on.

"Life sucks. People let you down. Sometimes we even let ourselves down. I don't think you need a ring to remind you of that. It'll only hold you back."

His steely gaze drops to my left hand where my wedding ring remains. He says nothing. He doesn't need to, because that hard stare says it all.

I'm one to talk.

Giving up, I leave him by the waterfall to battle his demons in private as I head home to my ghosts.

Chapter Five

Lee

They say ignorance is bliss. I say it's just ignorant. I'm always aware of what's going on around me and aware of things most others just overlook.

"Man, if you want me to do something around here, I'm only going to agree to do it the right way. No half-a— umm, no half-tailing it."

Chase stands beside me with his arms crossed in a mirror image of my pose, both of us studying the peeling paint of the church window and door trims. He unfolds a hand and motions toward the trim. "You sure we can't just paint over it?"

"Not if you want it to look decent. When I pressure washed it the other day, I got what I could off. Now I need some sandpaper and maybe paint remover." I go over what other supplies I need to strip the old paint and the process to prep it for a new coat.

Chase finally nods his head. "If you're up for the challenge."

"I am. I've already texted the list of supplies to Drew. He'll be here shortly."

Chase gives me a look I can't decipher. "Okay. Just turn your receipt in to Bellamy."

"No worries. I've got it." I wave the idea off.

"Your community service is to serve, not pay." He stuffs his hands into his khaki pants pockets and rocks back on his heels.

I look at the old church building. It's clean on the inside and cared for, but showing its age. "Why haven't you had maintenance and repair work done before now? Is the church hurting for money or something?"

"The church has plenty of money. We just choose to put it back into the community through outreach programs and ministry. The building has only recently gotten overlooked. My brother Beau was better at keeping that kind of stuff in check." Chase looks away and I don't know why it's taken weeks for me to put two and two together, but suddenly something becomes clear.

"Your brother and Bellamy's husband are one and the same?"

He nods, and, after a few beats, clears his throat. "Well, if you need anything else I'll be inside." He's gone before I can come up with something to say.

While I wait on Drew to show up with the supplies and some food, I go check on No-tail. A vet came out and examined the cat, concluding the tail was gone and not coming back. He thought he was funny. I did not. The patch of missing fur was probably scraped off during whatever accident the cat survived and will eventually grow back. The vet declared the cat male and basically healthy, gave me a tube of ointment for the furless patch, put a flea collar on him, and left me paying a ridiculous bill. Not that I'm strapped for cash.

"Yo, No-tail. How's it swinging?" I say, bending down to pet him. He lets out a meow in reply to our inside joke.

"Aww, ain't this so cute and cozy."

I look over my shoulder and find Neena grinning at me, all googly eyed. "Well, if it ain't my favorite person, Neena Busybody... What's your last name now?"

"Reed. Middle name is actually *Saint* or *Lee's Guardian Angel*."

"Whatever, smart-aleck." I stand up to face off with the pint-sized woman. "I really don't like you anymore. What gave you the right to get up in my business?"

"I'm not one to sit back and watch people destroy themselves. I think it's time you stop acting like a bratty teenager and start being a respectable grown man. What are you, thirty something?"

"Thirty-four, and I've formed a multimillion-dollar company from the ground up, sweetheart. I'm most definitely a grown man."

"Respectable though?" She taps the toe of her cowgirl boot against the cement floor, sending out an echo around the garage as she levels me with a look.

"You here to call me names, or is there something else you need?"

I catch a glance of Bellamy moving toward us in a short yet baggy dress with leggings underneath. Would it kill the woman to show just a glimpse of those long legs?

"I brought you cereal." Neena opens a cloth grocery bag and pulls out a giant-sized box of Captain Crunch, reminding me of our grocery store rendezvous down the cereal aisle a long time ago. I came on to her and she turned me down. Just like her sister, making me conclude they are the only two decent women God ever created. Too bad I can't talk either one of them into being mine.

"Where's Rambo?" I ask, deflecting my thoughts away from women in general.

"Asher is on the way. We have a counseling session with Pastor Chase in about thirty minutes, but I wanted to stop by and check on you first." Neena clutches the box of cereal to her chest with one hand and waves at the approaching Bellamy with the other. A group of old men wiggle their way out of a variety of vehicles and stop her before she gets to us.

I cross my arms and smirk down at Neena. "Trouble in paradise already? That was quick for you newlyweds."

Neena shakes her head while her cheeks turn pink. "It's not that type of counseling. It's... We're working through some PTSD issues." Her answer slaps the smirk off my face.

I suck in a deep breath, wishing it were that easy to pull my asinine remark out of the air, and reach over to give her tiny shoulder a squeeze. "Neena, I'm sorry. That's nothing to joke about."

Her husband fought and almost died for our country, and she's done her fair share of rescuing innocent lives while putting her own life at risk. They're both heroes and I shouldn't be giving her any lip. It makes me wonder what's wrong with me. Sometimes the inability to keep my mouth shut makes me really hate myself.

Neena leans closer. "But if our marriage were in trouble, that would be nothing to joke about either."

She had to go there.

I snort out a derisive chuckle and roll my eyes. "Come on, sweetheart. You know as well as I do the sanctity of marriage in this country is nothing but a joke. People toss vows out there just to wax poetic with no real convictions behind it."

"Wow. Cynical much?"

"I just call it like I see it."

"Then your vision is quite a sad one. No wonder you're self-destructing." Neena slaps the box of cereal against my chest and goes to speak to Bellamy, who's been surrounded by the old men like Snow White with her hunchbacked dwarves.

I toss the box onto the workbench and lean against the doorframe, watching in astonishment as Bellamy's face transforms. In the last month, I've only seen anger and sadness etched along the sharp contours of her face. Before me now, the woman just blossomed. One of the old geezers said something to make her smile, and I feel that smile all the way to the pit of my stomach. First instinct is to figure out how to make her do that myself, but then I dismiss that stupid thought. I glance down at the pinky ring for a distraction, only to look back up when the group lets out a string of laughter.

And… she's still smiling.

Man, is that one beautiful woman. She catches me watching her, sending that veil of scorn to snap back into place. Yeah, she might be beautiful, but too bad she also has a mean streak as long at the Tennessee River.

Bellamy says something to the group, sending all eyes toward me. Waving, she leaves them and heads over to me. She releases a long sigh as she steps inside the garage. "Until Drew gets here, Chase wants you to work on weeding the flowerbeds around the fellowship hall."

"Okay." I search for something to put the weeds in, but not before noticing the same disbelieving expression she wears every time I agree to do whatever menial task she divvies out. "Look, Belle, I'm not afraid of hard work. Done it all my life."

"D-don't call me that," she stutters. "My name is Bellamy."

I grab the nearest bucket and walk past her. "Belle suits you."

She's stays right on my heels. "No, it doesn't, so don't."

"Yes, it does. You're beautiful. A true belle." My inability to let it go even though it's clearly upsetting her makes me cringe again.

I wait for her comeback but only get a sniffle before she storms inside the church. Royally ticking off two women within a span of ten minutes is a new record for me. Not one I'm proud of, so I choose to leave her alone and go pull weeds like an obedient prisoner.

"Good day, kid," an older man says as he walks past where I'm kneeling by the door.

"Hey," I mumble, plucking a weed with one hand.

"Hi there. I know you," another geezer says after a few minutes.

I glance up and see him strutting to the door with a walking cane in one hand and a pot of something in the other. "Hey, sir."

"I really like those bike-build specials you do on the Discovery Channel."

"Thank you." I swat at a fly buzzing around my ear and focus back on the weeds. The stubborn one in my fist fights back by poking tiny thorns into my palm. The sudden sting serves as a reminder of my downward spiral that landed me on the side of the road in a mangled mess. I can't believe I allowed myself to get that out of control. Disgusted with myself for not being stronger, I squeeze the weed until the thorns bite deeper into my skin.

"That your motorbike in the garage?"

A glance over my shoulder finds him still standing there, so I dump the prickly weed into the bucket. "Yep."

"Got some work ahead of ya, but nothing you can't handle, right?"

"The tranny is cracked so that'll need replacing, and the gas tank will have to be refabricated from scratch, but yeah, it's fixable."

"My name's Jeb. If you need a hand, just let me know. Back in my day, I rebuilt a motor or two."

I stop weeding to get a good look at him. A lanky old guy with wisps of white hair that aren't enough to conceal the shine of his bald head, but Jeb has that air of arrogance that lights a man who knows what he's talking about. "I may take you up on that."

Jeb tips his head and leaves me alone. Several more old men shuffle past, offering various greetings, making me curious about why they're meeting. Not curious enough to stop weeding to find out though. The quicker I weed, the quicker it'll be done.

After dumping the bucket in the woods, I walk to the other side of the fellowship hall to knock those beds out. The windows are open and a delicious scent hits me as I bend down to get started. Cackling and chattering reach me as well. I pop my head up and peer inside.

About a dozen or so men surround a cast iron pot as if it holds a secret potion. I've not had breakfast yet, so whatever it is sure does smell good. Taking my eyes off the pot, I give the group a onceover. They could have stepped right out of a Huckleberry Finn book. A ragtag group of various races and sizes, wearing anything from overalls with John Deere trucker hats to tweed jackets and newsboy caps. They remind me of a bunch of mischievous boys, but with wrinkles and graying hair.

A pudgy man glances up from the pot before I can duck away. A wide grin breaks out on his round face. "Hey there, sonny. Come here and help us decide something."

A quick glance around finds neither of my wardens are in sight. "I better stick to weeding this flowerbed."

"Nonsense. Chase won't mind if you help us out. It won't take long."

I case the side entrance to the church again, stomach winning out over my better judgement. "Uh, sure, but I gotta hurry."

A table holding a selection of pots comes into view when I open the back door. As I join them, a black man wearing his tweed cap on backwards scoops a serving of golden yellow grits into a bowl. He presses a plastic spoon into my hand before I have time to protest. "Taste 'em and tell us what you think."

I dip the spoon into the bowl and give it a sniff before taking a bite. The grits are extra creamy but just this side of too salty. "Good, but the salt could be toned down."

"I told you, Harvey." The pudgy one points to the guy who gave them to me.

"Then let Lee try yours, Clarence, if you think yours are so much better." Harvey glares at him.

Each old man pushes a bowl of grits on me in succession until my gut is nicely full. They take their grits seriously. From their comments, it appears they take all food seriously. While I'm taste-testing, I discover these guys call themselves the Valley Church Men's Group.

"So you guys hold a cooking competition each week under the guise of Bible study." I point to the unopened Bibles scattered on one of the tables.

"We eventually get to the Bible study after we eat and have social hour," Jeb answers, still close to my side.

"Social *hour*? How long do y'all hang out here?" Someone will be looking for me soon, so I ease toward the door to make my escape.

Clarence rubs his chubby cheek and shrugs. "Just a couple of hours."

"Ain't like we got much else going on besides lunch, afternoon naps, and the evening news," Harvey admits.

"Well, this has been real." I pop my flat but quite full stomach. "But it's time for me to get back to work. Thanks, guys."

"Just so we're clear, my grits won, right?" a little man wearing a plaid shirt and denim overalls asks. I think his name is Wade.

"Hands down. Put bacon in something and it'll always be a winner." I clamp a hand on his shoulder and his face lights up. These old men are easy to please.

"Come back next Tuesday and help us decide who makes the best breakfast casserole," Jeb says as I start to open the door.

"Yeah. This has been the best judging we've had in a long while," Harvey adds.

"I agree. Beau was always honest like you, but Chase just pacifies us by saying it's all good. And the preacher is getting a little thick in the middle, so maybe it's time we give him a break." Wade makes a face.

"I sure do miss Beau. He told the best jokes." The mood in the room changes with Clarence's statement. "You know any jokes, Lee?"

I shake my head. Sure, I know some, but none appropriate enough to share with this group.

"That kid could light up a room," he adds with a long sigh. Each old man visibly deflates and murmurs various sentiments. Now I wish I would have made a run for it when I had the chance. They set in to telling a few Beau stories as I keep trying to figure out a way of escape. *Beau was the youth pastor... Beau did missionary work overseas each year... Beau led local homeless ministries...*

"You would have liked him, Lee. Beau was a man's man and made time for us ole fogies like we really meant something to him." Harvey's eyes start to water.

"How could you guys not mean a lot to him? You're a standup bunch..." Clearing my throat, I change the subject, "What time should I meet y'all next Tuesday, so I can clear it with Chase?"

Just like that, down-turned mouths reverse and faces are beaming.

"Nine!" Clarence shouts with a little too much enthusiasm. "Bring your appetite."

"You can count on it. And I'll see if I can round up some jokes. See you guys then." I tuck tail and get out of there before they pull me in for another round of conversation. My mind is already refocusing on the bucket of weeds again, but I come to a halt when I notice Bellamy sitting on a bench just out of sight from the open windows. Judging by the expression on her beautiful face, she heard every word.

She follows me all the way to the edge of the woods where I dump the weeds. "It's best if you leave those guys alone. I won't have you disappointing them."

"How can I disappoint them? It's just tasting food for crying out loud." Needing some relief from the itch forming underneath my cast, I unfasten the bucket handle and straighten it before shoving one end inside the cast. The wire hits the right spot, sending my eyes rolling and me releasing a satisfied moan. It's then that I notice Bellamy is talking.

"They get attached, and we both know you won't be here long, and losing people is hard and it's best to just never get attached in the first place..." Bellamy keeps rambling basically the same thing over and over, offering another glimpse of that hurt she's carrying around.

It's on the tip of my tongue to smart off about her being the one with issues and not the old men, but somehow I keep from slinging it out there. For the first time in forever, I really don't want to use my words as a repellant, but for something else. I lower my voice and say, "Beau sounded like a great guy."

Bellamy stutters out a breath. "The best." There's so much pain in those two whispered words that I almost wrap my arms around her to see if I can lessen it. This woman is cut from a different cloth than any I've encountered, though. My embrace would probably only add to her burden.

"I promise I won't disappoint them."

Her chin quivers as she dips her head, and that movement does something to me. The long waves of black satin curtain her face, and it takes all my willpower not to tuck a strand behind her ear.

She sniffs. "Please keep that promise."

"Bellamy," I rasp, causing her to look up. Those gold eyes collide with mine.

The tension presses down on us, like the humidity has suddenly grown to stifling. I reach for her, but my hand retreats at the last minute. She wouldn't like me touching her, but man, do I want to. This is also new—denying myself something I could easily take.

After a few more heavy moments pass, she leaves me by the line of trees and marches back to the church. Seems it's her mission to put space between us.

I stand here and watch each and every step she takes, thinking 1 may be the one getting attached and ending up disappointed.

Chapter Six

Bellamy

The Sunday offering has been a disappointment for both Chase and me. My expectation was that the members would have a conniption about a convict collecting their money, but for some reason their response has been more on the lines of star-struck.

"The offering has gone up by fifteen percent just so people can get near the *almighty* Lee Sutton. I've never seen folks so eager to load the plates. Everyone seems to forget the reason why he's here in the first place." I huff, crossing my arms as I pace around Chase's office early Monday morning.

"No one has forgotten, Bellamy. Don't you want visitors to walk through the doors of our church and be greeted with open arms?"

"Yeah... If he feels so welcome then why does he slip out the back door as soon as the offering is done?" This is the part that hasn't met Chase's expectations. My brother-in-law actually thought Lee would sit on the front pew and be praising Jesus within minutes. Wonderful and great in theory, but that's not the real world.

"It's only been six Sundays. We have at least thirty more to go. I have faith Lee will come around." Chase offers a confident smile—a smile so similar to his brother's that my heart squeezes.

"So you're pulling out with the deacons?" A glance at the clock indicates it's a little before six in the morning. "You need anything before you go?"

53

"Leaving in about ten minutes, yes, but I think I have everything I need. Thanks though. The conference wraps up Wednesday. You think you can hold down the fort until then?" Chase packs his briefcase while cutting me a look.

What he really wants to know is if I'll be nice to Lee, since he's under the impression that I wasn't so nice Friday. Lee's minions—six of them this time—showed up with a giant grill and a butchered hog at seven in the morning. What Lee called a business luncheon ended up being a rowdy gathering of burly men who played their heavy metal music too loud while hanging out and working on putting his smashed bike back together. The parking lot looked like a bike show with an entire line of Sutton Custom bikes on display. Drew, who has found a voice in the last few weeks since we see each other on an almost-daily basis, was quick to brag on that fact.

When Judge Pruitt arrived at my request, he deemed what was happening as work and left me with a smirking Lee Sutton. I may have showed out a little, playing the fun police by checking all the coolers (where only bottles of sodas were discovered) and then constantly telling them to turn the music down.

Even the Men's Group showed up for the "business luncheon" with side dishes and gallon jugs of sweet tea. Lee was a gracious host and allowed Clarence to switch the music to the Eagles and other classic rock. Later, Harvey had his request met with tunes from BB King.

Of course, I was stuck supervising the little party due to Chase and Rebecca taking the new youth pastor and his wife out to dinner. While I know it's nothing personal and the church needs a new youth pastor, it's starting to feel like everyone is moving on without me and Beau. *You're still living*, whispers through my thoughts. *It sure doesn't feel like it*, I whisper back.

Shaking those dismal thoughts away, I place the offering summary on Chase's desk and tug on the hem of my tank top. "I can handle things while you're gone. If you're done giving me a hard time, I'm going to get my run in before the prince wakes for the day."

Chase chuckles. "Come on, Bellamy. He's not that bad. Have you noticed all the stuff he's fixed around here? The weed eater, the stove in the fellowship hall, the seesaw on the playground... He fixed my car. Said there was some issue in the steering. I have no idea how he even knew there was an issue with it. The man is like a mechanical savant."

"Yeah, sure." I manage to suppress an eye roll while I wave off the impending speech on why Lee Sutton is an amazing but misunderstood person. "I'll see you Wednesday."

I'm out the door and on the old track within minutes, easily finding my stride. Four laps is a mile, so I plan to make at least twelve rounds within thirty minutes. Three laps in, my mind wanders to this situation with Lee. The man has a way of making me feel exposed. He's not made a pass at me since his first day here and has only called me a handful of ugly names under his breath, but the way he watches me with those deep-blue eyes... It's the same intense attention he gives each project while trying to figure out how to fix it, but he needs to realize I'm not a project he can fix.

I try to refocus on the track. When the small rec center closed beside the church, the trustees thought it was a good idea to purchase the property. Beau and I took on the project of turning the rec building into a youth center and that's proven itself a great choice. The children enjoy riding their bikes or skateboards out here, and some of us like to run or walk laps, even though a resurfacing is past due.

One of the potholes is coming up, and in my attempt to sidestep it, distraction causes me to mistime it by a step.

And down I go.

Pain clamps down on my right ankle as I land on my hands and knees. Swallowing down the yelp, I roll to a sitting position. Before I can pull myself together, strong arms gather me up.

"Put me down!" I buck against Lee's chest.

"You're hurt." Lee strides toward the garage with his good arm wrapped around my lower back and the broken one underneath my knees.

Inhaling sharply to unleash a hissy fit, I catch a good whiff of him and stall. The man smells like a forest dotted with sandalwood. Trying not to bury my nose against his neck to get a better whiff, I grit out, "You're hurt worse. Put me down."

Lee grunts in response but keeps moving until he pushes through the side door and deposits me on a brand-new leather sofa in the corner. I protest, but he ignores me and works on gently undoing my sneaker before sliding it off my foot. His fingers smooth over the tender area at my ankle. "I'm gonna grab some ice from the fellowship hall. Sit tight."

I watch him stride out, knowing more protests will only fall on deaf ears, so I bite my lip to staunch the need to lash out at him or cry from embarrassment. While I try to calm down, my eyes scan the clean and orderly garage and stop on a fancy weight bench and a giant rack of free weights. A mat is rolled up and leaning against it, and above a giant flat-screen TV is mounted on the wall.

Lee's back in no time, and without saying anything, he props my foot with a pillow and places the bag of ice against my ankle.

"How'd you even know I fell?" I ask instead of thanking him like I should.

Lee looks around the room, his sharp cheeks actually coloring before my eyes. "I uh... I saw you from my window. There's a good view of the track from up there." Sighing, he sits on the arm of the couch.

I don't want to think about him up here watching me, so I change the subject. "You've made yourself at home, I see." I motion toward the exercise equipment. He's even set up a work space on the right where two bikes sit in various stages of completion.

"Figured I'm stuck here, so I might as well." He pats the cast on his arm. "Drew is coming by in a little while to remove this thing, so I need to get back to my workout routine." He leans over and adjusts the ice bag, which is starting to slip.

"Shouldn't a doctor be doing that?"

"Nah. The kid removed my stitches a few weeks ago with no problem. He's watching a YouTube video on how to do this, too."

"That poor guy does everything for you, short of wiping your nose." I cluck my tongue. "I sure hope you pay him well."

Lee snorts. "Trust me, the punk gets paid plenty. Plus, I'm teaching him how to build bikes."

"Oh…" I glance at him after readjusting the ice bag and notice his damp hair glitters in one spot with suds. "You still have some shampoo in your hair." I point to the left side of his head.

Lee yanks his shirt off and starts rubbing it against his hair. "I'm over this one-handed mess, and I'm taller than the showerhead. It's ridiculous." He shakes his head and huffs. "My bathroom at home is bigger than this entire garage. I feel like a giant stuck in a dollhouse upstairs."

I don't retort or huff, or breathe for that matter. My eyes freeze on his bare torso and how it tapers into a long waist, void of any ink.

"Hey." Lee snaps his fingers, causing my eyes to snap up in time to catch the smug look on his face.

Clearing my throat, I comment, "Your side has healed."

Lee touches his fingertips to the darkened skin before wrangling his shirt back on. The effort makes his abs flex. "Yeah. It's gonna scar, but I'll survive it."

I'm not sure how much longer I can survive lying on this couch, so I sit up and try putting weight on my foot. "It doesn't hurt too badly. I'm gonna head home and get ready for the day."

He catches my elbow even though I'm steady. "You sure?"

"Yeah. It's just a little tender." I scoop up my shoe and try making a getaway.

"That track is in bad shape." He holds the door as we step outside.

"I know. It was discussed at our last finance committee meeting, but nothing was decided." I squint, noting the dark clouds moving in over the mountain tops. "Looks like an inside workday. I'll have the carpet cleaner delivered so you can knock out the sanctuary."

Lee walks me all the way to the truck with his eyes fastened to my bare foot the entire time, then helps me climb inside even though I'm perfectly capable.

"I'll… I'll see you in a little while." I buckle the seatbelt and decide to offer him an olive branch. "I started a crockpot of my special oatmeal before botching my run. You want me to bring you a bowl?"

Lee redirects his attention from my ankle to my eyes. The concerned look vanishes as his lips twitch. "Does it have cinnamon and other spices?"

"Yes…"

He licks his lips and hums a small groan. "I love spicy stuff. Sure, babe."

Ah, and there it is—his arrogant act is back in place for some reason. I guess ten minutes of being a decent human was pushing it.

"*Bellamy*," I stress before shutting the door on whatever haughty words he was preparing to fire back. I put the truck in reverse and make the mistake of looking over only to see him wearing a full-on grin. "Jerk," I mouth as I drive past him, even though I'm beginning to think that's just an elaborate ruse to keep people at arm's length.

Hours later, I keep finding myself smiling at the empty container sitting on my desk. The man practically licked the bowl. Redirecting my attention once again to the computer screen, I work on the church bulletin while the droning of the carpet cleaner drifts in from down the hall. I hate to admit it, but Lee Sutton is one hardworking man. He gives me a good bit of lip about each task, but he executes each one of them like it's his mission.

My cell phone rings, catching me getting off track again. I pull it out of my top drawer and cringe at the name flashing on the screen, knowing if my lawyer is calling, it has something to do with Carl Waverly.

"Hello, Mr. Halbrook," I answer with a good bit of hesitance.

"Ah, Mrs. McCoy. How are you doing, dear?"

"Fine, I guess. And you?" I lean back in my chair and stare at the ceiling as the carpet cleaner turns off, leaving the office in an unsettlingly quiet.

"Good…" He releases a long sigh. "I've received another letter for you."

"And you know I don't want it." My heart starts thumping harder. I swivel my chair around and gaze at the wedding picture of Beau and me tucked on the bookshelf.

"I know, but… Bellamy, dear, I think you should at least see what he has to say."

"That man killed my husband," I mutter, nearly choking on the words. "What could he possibly have to say that can make that any better?"

"I understand, but reading them may help give you some closure."

Carl Waverly has written me a total of twenty-six letters over the last two years, each one delivered to my lawyer's office where they remain. The pain that has ebbed a little lately crawls back up my spine and claws at my shoulders and neck. "Don't sling the word *closure* at me. There's no such thing. Waverly got drunk and used his car as a deadly weapon against my husband. His letters won't give Beau back…" A sob escapes and my vision blurs.

"Bellamy—"

Sniffing back the tears, I interrupt, "Look, I appreciate you letting me know, but I need to go. Goodbye." I hang up before he can try talking me into it again.

A throat clears by my open door, sending a cringe to accompany the discomfort in my shoulders. Wiping my eyes, I turn the chair. By the look on Lee's stoic face, there's no doubt he heard every word. We say nothing for a spell, just keep our eyes locked on each other. He's clear across the room, but I can feel the weight of his stare as it roams my face.

"Come here," Lee orders.

"You don't boss me—"

"Could we just *not* for a minute?" It's the statement we've started using when the other wants to drop the snarky pretenses for a moment and just be real. Lee points in front of him and repeats slowly, "Come here."

Tentatively, I stand and round the desk until reaching the spot in front of him. "What?" I ask without looking up at him, focusing on the collar of his dark-blue T-shirt instead.

He answers by wrapping his arms around me and pulling me against his chest. Stunned, I stand frozen with my arms to my side. So stunned, in fact, my tears have disappeared and all I can do is bask in his warmth and strength. It's such a luxury after going so long without affection that I have to fight to keep from breaking down.

The wall clock ticks off several rounds before I find my voice. "What are you doing, Lee?"

"I'm holding you together," he whispers close to my ear. "And it would work a lot better if you'd hold me back."

I've never heard someone refer to a hug as *holding you together*. It's an odd way of putting it, but it makes the embrace more significant. Every cell in my body says to do as he suggested and hold him back, but my mind is muddled with grief from the phone call and confused as to why I'm enjoying another man holding me.

"I can't..." I wiggle and push against his chest until Lee drops his arms.

"Bellamy?"

I turn to the desk, my hands gripping the edge to keep from shaking. "Are you done with the floors?"

"Yes."

"Then let's just call it a day." I keep my back to him, expecting him to storm off while muttering a few choice words. Instead, he steps closer and surprises me by running his fingers through the back of my hair. He only does it once, but it's enough to overwhelm me completely.

"I read somewhere once that forgiveness doesn't excuse their behavior. Forgiveness prevents their behavior from destroying your heart." Lee combs his fingers through my hair one last time before leaving me trembling with indignation, because I know he's absolutely right.

Chapter Seven

Lee

Sundays have been a drag. It's the only day I've ever allowed myself to sleep in, but this ridiculous sentence has me up early and dressed decent enough to take people's money.

The idea of me doing this could be viewed as funny, and maybe one day I'll look back on this and have myself a good ole chuckle, but there's no humor to be found about it presently. From the sour look on Bellamy's face, she agrees.

I reach her pew and pass the offering plate while arching an eyebrow when I catch her eye. She answers with a subtle shake of her head. I let it go and move to the next pew, ready to be done with this so I can go put in a workout, but I can't get Bellamy out of my head. She looked close to tears and that does something peculiar to me. She's on a sinking ship, like the one she rescued me from just yesterday, so there's no option but to climb aboard with her.

I hand off the offering plate to one of the real ushers and move back to her pew, then motion for her to scoot over so I can sit at the end just in case I need to bail on this idea.

"Hey," Bellamy protests.

"Hi," I reply brightly, earning a daggered glare from the beauty. I don't care though, because I owe her.

My agent showed up with one of the producers from the network yesterday, insisting I agree to them shooting a special on my current situation. I'm not into reality TV trash and that's all the special would turn into, so I told him as much and followed that with a hard no. The gossip magazines have cashed in on my stupidity, and now my agent and network want to do the same. The entire time we were arguing back and forth in Chase's office, Bellamy was at the desk typing away. When my agent handed over my contract and pointed out where I wasn't allowed to say no, Bellamy hopped up and excused herself.

She was back within minutes, waving my file in the air. "It clearly states in his file from the judge that Mr. Sutton is not allowed to be filmed. That includes interviews and TV specials." She looked serious as a heart attack while handing it over for them to read, but I knew it was total bull.

Once they left, I called her out on it. "Now that's a true lie."

She scoffed. "No... The paper was in your file. That wasn't a lie. They didn't need to know I added it moments before walking back in here with it." She winked one of her gorgeous gold eyes and it made my heart skip a beat. No joke, the sucker had to pause.

"Why'd you go through all that trouble for me earlier?" I asked her later while she helped me feed the cat—which was unnecessary but I kept that to myself.

"I'm your guardian, and as long as you're in my care, it's my job to look out for your best interest."

It's not her job and we both know it. She earned a point in my book for that, so for no other reason than needing to look out for her as well, I'm willing to endure this church service.

"Good morning, everyone," Chase says, pulling my attention up to the pulpit. "So glad y'all have joined us this fine September morning. Today, we want to officially welcome our new youth pastor, Mark Tyler, and his lovely wife Jocelyn to our Valley Church family."

A young couple stands up from the front pew and turns to smile and wave at the congregation. I look at Bellamy out of the corner of my eye and see her fighting to keep it together. Oh, man, now her mood makes perfect sense. The Men's Group was especially chatty about Beau and Bellamy this past Tuesday, talking about all the couple did for the youth group, while they shoveled various types of cornbread into my mouth.

Instinctively, I start to put my arm around Bellamy to shield her, but I stop myself. Instead, I move closer until our arms and legs touch. I hope it makes a clear statement to her that I have her back. When she doesn't move away from my touch, I think it does.

There's singing and a message, but I couldn't tell you what it was about, because I'm too hyperaware of Bellamy coming close to falling apart. It's like she's battling this internal war that no one is looking close enough to see, but I see it and am ready to catch her if need be.

"After closing prayer, I'd like to invite everyone over to the fellowship hall for a covered dish dinner to celebrate the Tylers joining us," Chase announces before appointing some guy to lead us in the prayer.

I lower my head and close my eyes but snap them open when I feel Bellamy practically climbing over me to get out of the pew. Knowing she wouldn't want me to chase her, I stay put and let her go. By the time I make it through this overly friendly crowd to get outside, her truck is gone.

There's nothing I can do now that she's gone, so I pass the day with a vigorous workout, focusing on my left arm, and manage to rewire a bike one of the guys dropped off for me to finish up. This eats up some hours, but there's still too much free time with Bellamy heavy on my mind. Feeling restless close to dark, I gather up some supplies in a backpack, slide on a pair of flip-flops, and hike over to the waterfall to shower. The icy pelts of water are close to painful, but I welcome the sensation, along with the space to actually wash and rinse properly. Not wanting to get caught, I only linger long enough for my skin to grow numb before getting out, dressing in a pair of lounge pants, and hauling it back to the garage.

I leave the side door open to let in some of the fresh air for No-tail before climbing the stairs and stretching out on the bed. I want the cat to know at least one of us is free to come and go, but he seems content just hanging around here.

Wanting to check on Bellamy but not really sure how to go about it, I text her a video of No-tail attacking a catnip ball from earlier. It's funny as all get-out. Without the tail, he looks like a big ole ball of fur tumbling around. The screen indicates she's read it, but she doesn't reply. Giving up on the stupid idea of cheering her up, I toss the phone on the mattress beside me and pick up the remote control.

The phone pings a message and startles me. Chuckling at myself, I pick up the phone but drop the smile when it indicates a message from Lance.

The judge still isn't wavering, stubborn old goat.

I don't even waste my time replying to that, just toss the phone down beside me and go back to channel surfing. The guy texts every other day with the same bull. I don't even care anymore.

Thing is, I've never backed down from doing what needs to be done. If holing up in this tiny apartment and being a glorified handyman is something I've gotta endure, then so be it. I'm over sulking about it and have actually realized it's not been so bad to have a break from myself. I was beginning to despise Mr. Motorcycle. It ain't me, and I don't even know when I morphed into that shallow idiot in the first place.

An hour later, I'm flipping through channels on the TV when I hear a soft knock on the door. Not sure if it's wishful thinking, but I'm pretty sure I know who it is before I open the door to see the sad beauty standing on the other side. The tip of her nose is red and those bewitching eyes are swollen, so there's no hiding how rough the day has been on her.

Bellamy's eyes are glued to my chest as she hitches a thumb over her shoulder. "I'm going to hang out with No-tail."

"Okay." I wait until she turns to head downstairs before tossing on a T-shirt and following behind her.

She settles on the couch and No-tail immediately hops into her lap. A light dusting of gray fur settles against her pink shirt, and it's all I can do not to reach over and start plucking the hairs off the fabric. To get my mind off it, I sit beside her and study the profile of her face. Straight nose, high cheekbones, a prominent bottom lip, sharp jawline, long, thick eyelashes... Yeah, God took his time creating this beauty.

The weight of my stare has to be felt, but Bellamy keeps her glassy eyes averted. Man, I wish there was a way to disassemble all the sad she carries and redesign it in with lots of happy as easily as I can remodel a bike. Shoot, wish I could disassemble a lot of things and remodel them to a healthier version. Like Gavin's health. My black heart.

I continue studying Bellamy's face, spotting a small beauty mark near the corner of her eye, and wait for her to say something. It doesn't take long for her to start talking, but it surprises me the direction she goes.

"What happened to your brother?"

I rub my chest, not liking the feeling she just slapped against it with that question. "Cancer happened."

Bellamy pets No-tail as she stares across the garage. "Care to elaborate?"

"I'd rather not..." I take a deep breath, catching the spicy scent she carries around, and slowly let it out. "It happened so fast. One day we were playing Tonka trucks and the next Tommy was in the hospital. In another blink, he was gone."

"What happened after that?" She stops petting the cat and briefly touches my forearm, maybe to encourage me to keep talking.

Stretching my neck side to side to release the tension there, I stew on the *after* for a minute or two. It was a lonely, confusing time where nothing felt right. Ma stayed in bed for weeks. Dad never came home. I even ran away for a couple of nights and hid out in a neighbor's treehouse until I finally got hungry enough to come home. Sad part is, no one ever noticed I was gone.

"Lee?" she asks, touching my arm again. Her fingertip grazes over Tommy's initials near my wrist. I had the tattoo artist use the bold Tonka logo font for it, knowing my little brother would have gotten a kick out it. He loved those bright-yellow trucks so much that I even slipped a mini one in his casket before they buried him.

My chest tightens even more. I want to eighty-six this conversation, but I can't ask her to share if I'm unwilling to do the same. "Ma eventually split. After she made it clear she wasn't coming back, Pop fell into a bottle for a few years. Then he sobered up and found himself a new family."

"Lee, that's terrible." Bellamy finally looks at me. Her pretty face is downturned with pity. I'd call her out on it, but I kinda pity her at the moment, too. "Who took care of you?"

"I did. Learned the lesson early in life that no one else will." I expect her to ask more, but she seems to realize she's pushed for enough.

We just sit in silence until No-tail jumps down and strolls off.

Bellamy turns so that she's facing me. "Can I tell you something?"

I nod.

"I miss being held. Beau... he gave the best hugs. And I didn't realize how much I missed them until you gave me one the other day."

I don't know what to say to that, so I say nothing.

"Lee, will you... Do you think it would be alright if..." Bellamy fumbles around with her words and starts to fidget. Huffing, she finally blurts, "Will you hug me?"

Such a simple thing to ask, but it feels far from simple and I've never wanted to give something more in my entire life. Again, I say nothing, just do as she's requested. I tuck her head against my chest, right where my heart is pounding hard enough she has to feel it. When she settles there on a long sigh, I give in and run my fingers through her soft hair.

"This doesn't mean anything," Bellamy whispers after a while. Her arms tighten a little more.

I tighten my hold too. "I know," I agree, knowing we're both lying. "Just tell me when it gets to be too much."

****

We have a new norm on Sunday evenings. I find something to tear apart and Bellamy hangs out with No-tail while I put it back together. She's not asked for any more hugs, and I'm both relieved and disappointed. Nothing has ever felt so right in my entire life as it did when I held her in my arms, but one glimpse of the pinky ring reminds me to keep some space between us. I won't risk letting another woman get away with walking out on me like my mother did.

"How do you even know how to fix that?" Bellamy asks. "You're not a carpenter."

I look up from the glider swing and shrug. "I don't, but once I take it apart and assess whatever is hanging up this left side, then I'll go from there."

She absently pets No-tail. "You make it sound like no big deal."

"It's not to me."

"How'd this even come about?"

"After Tommy died and my parents checked out, I needed an outlet. One day, I decided to smash every toy Tommy and I owned. By the time all the innards of a remote-control car were splattered all over the floor, I was intrigued with the idea of putting it back together."

"So, you fixed it?" She looks hopeful, but I shake my head.

"I gave it my best shot, but no. And that fail lit a fire under me. I was home alone a lot, so I started in on small appliances. An old hand mixer, the toaster, a blender. Once I figured out how to tear them apart and put them back together again, I moved on to the VCR and TV." I pull the arms off the glider and sit them in a line on a mat behind me. "Hand me the Phillips head screwdriver."

"Here." Bellamy taps me on the shoulder with it, and I have to smile when I see she's handed me the right one.

"How do you know about tools and stuff?"

"My dad is pretty handy, and Beau was all about trucks. I paid attention."

"Is that Beau's truck you drive?" I ask and look up in time to see her pretty face fall.

"It was his dream truck. A picture of it was his screensaver on his computer, and he had an old water cooler jug for all his loose change. Called it his dream truck fund. After he died—" A screw pings against the concrete floor and starts rolling off, but Bellamy scoops it up and places it in the bowl I'm using for the loose hardware. She sits beside me and starts fiddling with a hole in the knee of her jeans. "Anyway, most folks probably think it's frivolous and a waste of money, but I took the extra money from the life insurance and bought Beau his truck."

"No. I get it. That's one sweet truck. Bet he'd be impressed his woman fulfilled his dream." I nudge her leg, but she won't look at me.

"I hope so." She sniffles and then clears her throat, and I swear I can't figure out how to have a conversation with her that doesn't end up here.

I come up with a subject change on the fly. "You mentioned your dad. He around here?"

"No. He's a military man, so right now he and my mother are stationed in Washington State."

"Wow. That's a haul."

"Yeah." She sniffs again, indicating my subject change was a fail.

"There's no other family near?"

"I have the McCoys and Valley Church members," Bellamy mumbles. My questions come to a halt as I realize she's only getting more upset by the minute.

I drop the screwdriver and do something totally stupid without thinking it completely through. I maneuver both of us until I have her pinned underneath me before it even registers what I've done.

"What are you doing?" Eyes wide, Bellamy gasps and slaps against my chest but I don't move.

"You smell so good it drives me crazy..." I lean into her neck and skim my nose along it while she keeps pounding her fists against my chest. "Hmm... You smell *real*, babe."

"Get off me, you pervert!" She starts bucking underneath me, showing off that she's just as strong as I thought she would be. Man, this woman could give me a run for my money, which is probably why I decide to take this too far.

I push up and hover above her, reveling in the fury swirling in her liquid-gold eyes. Her full lips are pinched so severely that it's almost too tempting not to lean down and try to loosen them up with mine, but I refrain.

"Now you can't ever say you've not been underneath the *famous* Lee Sutton." I wink at her just before the left side of my face goes up in flames. I sit back on my haunches and rub the sting vibrating along my cheek as I watch her storm off. She sure knows how to deliver a proper slap.

"Jerk!" Bellamy shouts just before slamming my door.

That's okay. She can call me every name in the book. At least she didn't leave in tears this time. Dumb as it may sound, I count that as a win for both of us.

Chapter Eight

Bellamy

Lee Sutton is the most overwhelming man I've ever met. One minute he seems genuine and caring and then the next, he flips a switch. And that makes me flip a switch and act out in ways I've never done. Before meeting him, I have never raised my hand in anger toward anyone, but have already done it twice now within three months.

The arrogant man thinks he can treat people however he wants and can get away with it. It's time he realizes it's not right. I'm currently trying to convince Drew to climb aboard my bandwagon, but the young guy isn't budging past being completely loyal to Lee.

"You don't have to put up with his junk, ya know." I cross my arms and level him with a look while leaning back in my office chair.

Drew tugs on his long, white beard, eyeing me skeptically. "He only asked me to bring him some clothes. I ain't mad at it."

"Not even when he sent you away *twice* to retrieve other ones because you brought the wrong shirts?"

"He's picky." Drew shrugs and pulls out a sucker from what seems to be an endless supply. Always green and always smelling like apple.

"Why do you always have a sucker in your mouth?"

"Because Lee won't let me suck on a joint." He pops the sucker into his mouth, acting blasé about his bluntness.

I recover rather quickly and ask, "You always do what Lee tells you?"

Drew rolls the sucker from one side of his mouth to the other. "Might as well." He taps the community service log, reminding me to sign off on yesterday's work. He definitely looks out for Lee. Always popping in here to check that the log is up to date. "He just wants what's best for me."

"You sure about that?" I sign and date beside the six hours Lee worked on the playset refinishing.

"Don't let Lee fool you. The dude has a heart but doesn't want anyone to know it. He pretty much yanked me off the streets, made me go to drug rehab, and then moved me in with him until we headed here."

"Where do you live now?"

"Nosy much?" Drew snorts. "Lee had an apartment built at the back of his property for me and won't take a dime for rent either. I'm pretty sure I'd be dead by now had he not snatched a knot in my... backside."

I try not to smile, but it's hard not to be impressed with Lee and his crew for making an effort to clean up their language. "How'd y'all meet?"

Drew smirks and smooths a tattooed hand down the front of his Sutton Custom Bikes logo shirt. The shirt, a pair of low-slung Dickies with a wallet chain dangling, and steel-toe boots comprise his uniform. It seems to be what all of Lee's minions wear on a daily basis. "Lee caught me stealing one of his bikes. Broke my nose and busted my lip before sitting me down to lay out some rules on how it was going to be from there on out. Didn't even give me a choice. Just went about it." There's a lot of gratitude in his voice. "Seventeen and homeless in California, I didn't have any other options anyway."

"If he's so hard on you about drug abuse, then why is he out drinking and driving?"

Drew looks out my door as if he's preparing to make a run for it, but he steps closer to my desk instead. "Something happened to him when his nephew got sick a couple years back. Like he couldn't deal. Anyway, it's not my story to tell." He walks away at a clipped pace, making sure I comprehend this conversation is closed.

Right then, I understand Lee has earned his crew's loyalty. And of course, I feel bad for talking smack about him.

A loud beeping suddenly comes from the back of the church. Unable to place what it may be, I get up from the desk and head out to see what Lee has going on now. Really, it's almost daily that something is delivered or picked up. The man doesn't stay still.

I exit the side entrance but only find Drew's bike in the parking lot. The sound seems to be coming from behind the garage, so I walk around it and find a calamity of activity on the track at the same time the acrid odor of tar and smoke hit me.

Blinking my burning eyes, I scan the group of guys and easily spot Lee towering over them. He's pointing and directing as if he's the commander of the chaos. Even in a simple black T-shirt and faded jeans, the man exudes authority.

"What are you doing?" I yell at Lee over the noise of the equipment that is already pouring a layer of new surface on the track.

Lee finishes signing an invoice on a clipboard and hands it to a guy from the paving crew before turning to me. "I'm doing what Chase told me to do for today." He arches an eyebrow, daring me to dispute him.

He knows I'm going to regardless.

"No..." I wave a hand at the area in general. "Chase said for you to clean up the rec field so it'll be ready for the Harvest Day picnic. I'm pretty sure that meant picking up any trash and then mowing the grass."

"He wasn't specific, so I just went with my gut." Lee smirks, but then drops it when my fists ball up. "Look, this track was a lawsuit waiting to happen. It needed to be fixed and I had the means to do it."

"Our church does, too." I cross my arms.

"Yeah, well, now your church can put that extra money into more of those outreach programs."

"But—"

Lee leans closer and narrows his eyes. "You really gonna try to rob me of my blessing of donating this to your church?"

I lean back and fight my own smirk. "So, you were listening Sunday morning after all."

He scratches the dark stubble on his cheek, apparently trying to cover the fact that his lips are twitching. "Kinda hard not to."

"Admit it, worship service isn't so horrible." Ever since that Sunday the church welcomed the new youth pastor, Lee has stayed after taking up the offering to sit with me during services.

"As long as you're sitting by me, it's tolerable." He shrugs.

There's too much sincerity in that statement and my cheeks instantly warm from it.

"Let's get out of their way." Lee places a hand on the small of my back and leads us over to the garage where No-tail is peeping out the open side door.

Done sparring with him, I say, "Taking care of the track is really kind of you."

"Kind enough to earn me a favor?" His dark eyebrow arches once again, making him more handsome than should be allowed.

"Depends on what you want." Remembering the stunt he pulled in the garage, I take a step back and prepare for attack.

"Get your mind out of the gutter." Lee raises his palms. "My nephews want to come visit me this evening."

My shoulders relax. "I don't see why not. Sure."

"Great. Hang around though."

"Why?"

"Because I want them to meet you." He looks so sincere that I quickly agree.

"And, Lee..." I take a deep breath. "I want to apologize for slapping you."

Lee chuckles lightly and runs his fingers through his blond hair. "There's nothing to apologize for. Trust me. It's the most action I've gotten in almost three months." He follows that with a salacious grin and a wink.

And I follow that with a firm shove against his chest before storming off. "You just don't know when to quit, do ya?" I yell over my shoulder. His deep chuckle follows me all the way to the church.

Later, after running home to change into comfy jeans and a plain shirt, I make it back to the church with a container of fresh-out-of-the-plastic-tube cookies. I don't care what anyone says, they are delicious and I know the boys will enjoy them.

An hour passes while Lee allows the boys to tear apart a carburetor for the fun of it. Not sure if I'd consider that fun, but it seems to be working for them. I go about my usual routine of hanging out with the cat while I watch their progress.

Lee explained to me before their mom dropped them off that Gatlin and Gavin are eleven-year-old twins. Had he not said it, I would have never thought they were twins. Gatlin is a bit chubby in a typical healthy boy way with rosy, freckled cheeks, but Gavin is puny with shadows under his eyes and hollowed cheeks. The only characteristics they share are messy brown hair and big ole brown eyes. They are two cuties, but I don't dare tell them that since they are all of eleven years old and past the point of knowing how to take a compliment.

"Mrs. Mia is putting together another blood drive. You reckon you can come help me this time, Uncle Lee?" Gatlin asks as he inspects the bike Lee is currently working on, sounding like a grown fellow. "Working the crowd is a tough job."

Lee looks at me. "Gavin has an autoimmune disease, which makes him anemic. He's a patient at Mia's pediatric office and they put these blood drives together to support him," he explains before directing his attention to Gatlin. "I'm not sure, champ. I may still be here. When is it?"

"End of October," Gavin answers in his quieter voice from where he's sitting on the seat of the bike while Lee hovers close to him. It's a protective stance and another clue to the real man hiding behind the arrogant façade.

"The people here are really nice. I bet they'd let you go to it." Gatlin looks at me with hope brimming his eyes. "Won't you, Miss Bellamy?"

Lee grows anxious, rubbing the back of his neck and looking around for an answer that won't come to him.

"What if we had the blood drive here?" I blurt before stopping myself.

Lee blinks but then smiles. "You think that's possible?"

"Sure. I'll call Mia and see about scheduling it. We can serve fall-themed treats in the fellowship hall for the donors to enjoy afterwards. Oh, and I bet the youth group would like to take it on as one of their service projects."

"That'd be tight." Lee tips his chin up, trying to act tough even though his suddenly glassy eyes give away how much this means to him. "I'll handle all costs for it."

I come close to sassing him about always throwing money at things, but I've noticed his technique of throwing isn't to be seen doing it. No, Lee tends to lob it carefully at what he deems important when no one's looking.

"Sure thing. Let me see what I can come up with. In the meantime, who's ready for cookies and lemonade?"

Lee helps Gavin off the giant electric-blue and silver bike as both boys voice their agreements. He's more careful with his nephew than the expensive bike. Yet another point for Mr. Sutton. He's beginning to rack up quite a few.

Chapter Nine

Lee

The crowd lining up to give blood is impressive. Even more impressive than that is how Bellamy organized this thing out of thin air. I've watched her most of the morning while we've set up tables with all kinds of homemade treats covering them. There's no hiding the fact that she is in her element, directing youth to tasks and going over the schedule with the blood drive people. She's chill about it too. The woman never seems to sweat.

Wish I could be the same way, but I'm coming out of my skin and the brim of my hat is collecting a considerable amount of perspiration. I yank it off and mop my forehead with my shirt sleeve before shoving it low to give me a small shield from everyone.

"Why are you so antsy?" Bellamy asks as she breezes by me, trailed by a bundle of helium balloons. They're in an array of fall colors, like a tree going through the change—green, orange, yellow, and brown.

I follow her and the balloons until we are out of earshot from the crowd hovering over the food tables. "They all know why I'm here."

Bellamy ties the balloons to the back of a chair at the registration table and turns to give me a full-on unimpressed stare. "To support your nephews, yes." She begins shuffling through a stack of papers.

"No. You know what I mean." My eyes self-consciously sweep down my leg. Even though the dark-washed jeans conceal the monitor, it's like a jolt of awareness each time it taps the top of my boot, signifying how screwed up I really am. Most of these folks know I'm strapped to this place as tightly as a noose around some chum's neck, but they are all polite and slightly star-struck. Opposite of what I deserve.

"No one has mistreated you, have they?" Bellamy slides several pens into the pocket of her blue flannel shirt. She's multitasking, but I can tell she's still paying attention to what I'm saying.

Looking around when one of the kids calls my name, I wave at the teenage boy and give him a chin jerk. "No."

"You've been here almost four months and it's never bothered you before. Why now?"

"I don't know." I reach over and straighten one of the pens in her pocket, lining it up perfectly with the others poking out from the top. With her black hair tied in a high ponytail and the outfit of flannel, skinny jeans, and white Chucks, she looks as young as the youth she's been directing today.

"Seriously, Lee, what's the issue?" Bellamy asks, bringing my attention from her feet back to her eyes.

"I don't deserve their kindness or acceptance. I…" I pull the hat off again, comb my fingers through my damp hair, and shove it back on once again. The same weird feeling has followed me around all morning that usually worries me senseless during worship service. "I deserve their condemnation."

Being around Bellamy and watching her grieve, it's hit me hard lately that I could have easily killed someone's husband or significant other—or heaven forbid, a child—in my quest for self-destruction. I have no idea how the dude who killed her husband can even live with himself.

Bellamy steps close enough the spicy-sweet scent of her reaches me as she shoves a handful of brochure-looking things into my hands. "It's no one's place to play judge.

This crowd actually gets that, so get over yourself already and go help Gatlin give out donor pamphlets and stickers."

The only reply I can come up with is, "Yes, ma'am." I go find my nephew and try to shake the tension off my shoulders by focusing on him and our task of helping his brother and others in need of blood transfusions.

The afternoon rolls by until it's time for me to donate, so I join the line outside to the mobile blood bank. The cool breeze feels good after being cooped up in the fellowship hall for most of the day. I close my eyes and just focus on that sensation for a few seconds.

"Great," someone mutters from behind me.

I glance over my shoulder, but already know it's Bode Calder. "Yo." I give him a chin jerk and turn back around, not letting him think for a minute he's going to rile me.

We don't acknowledge each other during the ten-minute wait to get inside the mobile, but *luck* would have it we are placed side by side to donate.

Before the nurse can finish prepping, he's already going on and on about Mia after the nurse mentions knowing her. His continuous commentary on all things Mia and him is for my benefit and not the nurse's. It's *my baby this* and *my woman that.*

By the time she shoves the needle in my arm, I've had enough. "You've already claimed all that territory. Trust me, I get it. And I am not apologizing again, so knock it off," I tell him with as much attitude as I can muster.

"I don't recall an apology." Bode adjusts his glasses and squints at me. He reminds me of one of those outdoorsmen who live off the grid in his ratty shirt and cargo pants, but the glasses throw the look for a loop.

"No?" I ask, and he shakes his head. "I could have sworn I did… Anyway." I shrug and wait for him to whine about me still not giving one. It's as close as I'm getting to it, and he seems to realize it when he finally looks away.

Fact: I didn't cross any lines with his wife. Another fact: I would have in a heartbeat if Mia would have agreed. Yet another fact: I hate knowing this about myself.

"You guys are good bleeders," the blonde nurse comments. "You'll be done in no time."

I measure my bag with Bode's and see they are about even. That won't do, so I squeeze the squishy ball she gave me to see about hurrying this along. He catches on to what I'm doing and starts doing the same, eyeing our bags and squeezing the ball to death. We start pumping our hands like our lives depend on it.

"Guys, if you don't mind, please slow down." The nurse gives us a pleading look.

We listen but I smirk, knowing my bag is a little bit fuller than his. It doesn't take long to finish, so I wave the nurse to come back over so I can get out of here and away from the reminder of yet another mistake I was trying to cause with this punk's wife.

"I feel woozy," Bode mutters, sending another nurse over to check him out. He looks pale underneath that burly dark beard, but I give him no sympathy. "I'm seeing dots."

I chuckle as the nurse unfastens the needle and presses a cotton ball over the puncture wound. She instructs me to bend my elbow. The dude is over there whining the entire time, and I reach my limit on that as well.

"You're such a pansy." I stand up and am about to taunt him some more when someone turns out the lights...

The static in my ears slowly fades and my eyes open. It takes a few blinks to clear away the fog and realize I've somehow ended up back in the chair with a cool cloth pressed against my forehead.

"What happened?" I rasp before clearing the gravel from my throat.

"You acted like a pansy is what happened."

I tilt my head to the left and see Bode still laid out in his chair, too. "I haven't eaten anything this morning. Been busy helping Bellamy and your *baby* set this thing up."

"Whatever you say, man." Bode smirks like he has a right, but he looks as weak as I feel.

I take the cloth off my forehead and look around. "Where's everyone at?"

The nurse peeps her head from around the partition. "We're taking a fifteen-minute break."

"Oh."

"But I need you guys to relax for a little longer." Blondie walks our way with juice boxes and two plastic baggies with cookies inside. "Drink your juice and have a snack, then I'll see if you're okay to leave."

"Thanks," I say, taking her offerings.

"Holler when you're finished." After she hands over Bode's stuff, she disappears behind the partition again.

Bode snorts. "I can't believe you didn't hit on her with some lewd comment."

I chew on the sugar cookie and give his comment some thought. The nurse is a cute little thing, but there's no desire to flirt with her. That's weird, considering I'm going through the longest dry spell of my adult life. "I can't believe it either."

"What's up with you? Finally trying to be a standup man instead of a stupid punk?"

I shoot him a glare and almost crush the juice box in my fist. "I don't know who you think you are, but you might want to think twice before running off at the mouth to me."

"It was a compliment." He shoves another cookie into his trap, acting unperturbed.

"Funny way of putting it," I mumble between bites.

Bode slurps some juice. "Lee, there's nothing wrong with wanting to change for the better. Mia and I... Well, it took us some time to get over things with you, but we did and have been praying for you."

The bag falls into my lap. "Praying for me?" I ask and he nods. "For what?"

"We pray you'll get your life right with God."

"Look, I'm not in the mood for some religious talk." I crush the empty juice box, shove it in the bag with the remaining cookies, and swing my legs off the side of the chair to sit up. "I'm working on things. You said it, I've done some changing, but I know I'm not good enough for God, so let's just drop it."

We both stand at the same time in the cramped space, placing Bode in my personal space, which isn't flying with me. I fight the urge to shove him, taking a step back instead. A wave of dizziness rolls over me so I grip the back of the chair and wait for it to pass.

"Man, that's the thing. We can't do it on our own." Bode scoffs. "Do you even believe in God?"

"I ain't stupid. I know God's real. I don't need him all on my back to let me know it." I rotate my shoulders, which probably makes me look like a lunatic, but it feels like I'm under an attack of angry ants.

"Then why not turn yourself around and acknowledge God? Face him and stop being such a coward?"

Knowing I'm on the verge of totally losing it, I storm off as fast as my unstable legs will carry me. The entire mobile bank shakes from my hasty departure.

Truthfully, I don't know the answer to Bode's question. I was raised in church up until Tommy died, and then everything changed. I figured if my parents didn't want me then surely God didn't either. I was mad at Ma and Pop and ended up resenting God right along with them. No one wanted me, and I sure as life didn't want anyone either. I made my own way and it worked... until it didn't.

I dodge around the crowd in the fellowship hall until I find Bellamy at the refreshment table, loading a platter with plastic-wrapped brownies. She lifts her head and spots me.

"Hey. Do you want a brownie?" Bellamy holds up one of the thick chocolate squares.

"Nah. I'm not in the mood for sweets." I rub my eyes and then look around, the cookies churning in my gut.

"Things are winding down. You want to take a walk?"

And there Bellamy goes, offering me a lifeline once again. No matter how much I want to deny she's the reason I hurried in here, it's obvious.

"Yeah, okay." I follow her out the back door, and instead of heading to the waterfall like I expected, she leads me to the track where we start walking laps. Laughter and squeals from the playground reach us, but I keep my eyes averted from the large group of playing kids.

An entire lap passes with neither of us speaking.

"Do you want to talk about it?" She asks softly, nudging my arm.

I look at her briefly before focusing on the pavement. "Bode was just getting up in my business and it rubbed me wrong."

"How so?"

"He wanted to get all religious on me. I ain't about it."

"Bode isn't the type who gets all religious, so you're gonna have to sell this attitude another way."

I feel her looking at me, but I keep my eyes on my boots as I make long strides. "So him saying I need to give my life over to God ain't religious mumbo jumbo?"

"Sounds like the truth to me."

"Maybe," I mutter in agreement.

"God's not the enemy, Lee. Sin is. Take it from me. I went through a phase after Beau's death where I tried to blame God. But even then, I knew in my heart the blame was solely on Waverly and his sin."

"What's that got to do with me?" Feeling the need to hide, I step off the track and head into the woods, dodging a few low-hanging branches along the way.

"Everything," Bellamy says from behind me. "You told me I need to forgive the man who killed my husband, so that I can move on... Don't you think you need to forgive your parents for what they did to you, so you can, too?"

We reach what I consider my hiding spot. I stop at the edge of the waterfall and focus on the point where the water meets the top of the pool. "Bellamy, you can't give me this advice when you're not even using it yourself." I turn my head and meet her eyes. "What about you moving on?" I wave my arms around. "Seems we're both stuck."

Her eyes go liquid as she tries blinking back the moisture. "Does it count as effort if I'm starting to really want to try?"

"How are you going to try?"

Bellamy wraps her arms tightly around her middle. I want to pull her to me to give her the comfort she needs, but I've decided I'm not taking anything from this woman without her permission. She deserves that much respect.

"I picked up the letters Waverly sent to me," she whispers as if it's a secret.

"Yeah? Have you read them?"

She shakes her head. "No. I just can't bring myself to..."

We stare at the water, both lost in our screwed up heads, I suppose.

Bellamy settles on a boulder and draws her knees up. "I don't sleep well. Every night I go home and watch the video of Beau's last birthday until I pass out for a while. Then I get up in the mornings, come over here to run with hopes of clearing the haze away, and try pulling myself together enough to get through another day. It's robotic and all I can think about is getting back home to that video so I can hear my husband laugh again."

I sit beside her, feeling confused as to where this conversation went. I thought for sure I was going to get another religious speech like the one Bode gave me. That's another thing about this woman that draws me, she doesn't do the expected. I don't even know how to respond, so I remain mute.

"And if that's not pathetic enough, how about I have wished Waverly dead more than a handful of times." Her cheeks color.

Man, that sucks how she spends her evenings, but who could blame her for wishing the guy dead for what he did? I turn the conversation back to me before she falls apart. "I'm the pathetic one here."

"Pssh."

"Seriously. You don't read the tabloids? I'm a hellion." I huff and toss a loose rock into the water.

"I think you and the gossip rags don't give you enough credit."

"Well, that makes you the only one in a vast sea of many."

"That's your own fault, Lee. You don't let anyone see the real you."

I look over and get caught in her golden snares. "And who exactly am I?"

She shrugs, glances at the water, and then refocuses on me. "I'm not exactly sure, but I do know the man in the glaring spotlight is not the man sitting beside me. You're far enough away from the person in the headlines to make me want to discover the real Lee Sutton."

"No need. I'll only disappoint you."

Bellamy shakes her head. "There you go again, downing yourself. How can you pull off that arrogant, egotistical façade while feeling this way about yourself?"

"That façade is my repellant to keep people the heck away from me."

"But isn't that lonely?"

"It can be, but at least it's safe."

"Lee…" Bellamy places her hand on top of mine. "Is it worth it, though?"

I hate that this woman is beginning to make me doubt everything I've come to believe. Question every choice I've made. I'm about to pull my hand away when I feel her working the ring down my pinky finger. "Belle?"

She doesn't respond, just keeps sliding the ring off until it's pinched between her index fingertip and thumb. Her lips pucker and her eyes narrow as she scrutinizes it, turning the simple band one way and then the other. "I think you've held on to some blatant lies for too long, Lee. Letting them define you for no other reason than perhaps you being a little too scared to step up and be above the person you allowed people to shove into an ill-fitting box."

Before I can stop her, Bellamy tosses the ring toward the waterfall. "What the—"

"See." She motions to the water. "So insignificant that it didn't even make a sound hitting the water. Stop giving whatever is behind it so much power over you." Surprising me, she slides her wedding rings off, kisses the top of the diamond, and hands them to me. "Let's make an effort to move on from this point forward."

I weigh the pretty gold and diamond ring set in the palm of my hand before dropping them into her shirt pocket. They jangle against the pens still sticking out. "The sentiment wouldn't be the same, but I'm proud that you're brave enough to do it." I squeeze her shoulder before dropping my hand.

We hold each other's stare without saying anything else. The only noise is the rushing of water and the pounding of my heart in my ears.

Eventually, Bellamy blinks and looks away while rubbing her newly naked finger. "I need to get back to help clean up. Why... why don't you take a breather out here."

I nod, knowing she wants space from me, and watch her walk away. The boulder is backed up with a taller one, making a chair of sorts, so I lean against it, not caring to ever move from my spot. This hiding out in the woods is a little lame, but it's all the reprieve I'm allowed from life at the moment. I'll take it.

****

The day of the blood drive gave me more to think about than I wanted. Instead of focusing on me and my own issues that were pointed out, I focused on Bellamy's. Spending her evenings watching her dead husband on a video can't be healthy and that routine needs to be fixed. Not sure if it'll help, but at least a week's worth of research got my mind off of me.

I flip the hood of my jacket up to ward off the chill this morning and stand by the open bay of the garage, waiting for Bellamy to arrive for work. Like clockwork, the white truck slowly rolls in at eight.

"Yo, woman," I call out to her as she slides out of the truck. When she turns to acknowledge me, I motion for her to come over. "I have something for you."

Bellamy looks around the empty parking lot as if she's suspicious of me, but she walks over anyway. "Good morning, Lee."

"Hey, beautiful. How was your night?"

She eyes me and fiddles with the lapel of her suede jacket. It's a reddish purple and looks killer against her warm skin tone and gold eyes. "Okay, I guess."

All the answer I need to confirm it was as bad as always, but I let her get by with it and reach for the bag on the couch. "Here."

"What's this?" Bellamy peeps inside the bag.

"A book. It's by some Christian author from the south. Most of the reviews say she'll make you laugh, but I'm warning you, they also say she'll probably make you cry."

"I'm not much of a reader," she says, but takes the book out and inspects the cover.

"It never hurts to try something new, right?"

She flips through the pages even though there's no way she catches a word on any of them. "I suppose not... Thank you."

"No problem." I rub my palms together. "What's on the agenda for today?"

"How do you feel about sorting the food donations into boxes, so we can get them delivered?"

"Bring it." I wink and give her a lopsided smile.

Bellamy shakes her head and walks away while studying the book. Here's hoping she'll have a distraction for at least one night.

The deep rumble of a bike reaches me a few beats before Drew rolls up. He parks beside the garage and starts unpacking the saddlebags. "Yo. The light kit came in." He holds up a box, so I head over and help him carry the stuff inside.

"Everything good at the shop?"

"Yep."

"Did Ace get the Maverick bike shipped out?"

"Yep."

"You gonna say anything else besides yep?" I place the box on the workbench and cross my arms.

"Yep." Drew looks around.

"You looking for something?"

"Just making sure your little buddy isn't around."

I point at the cat sprawled out in his bed. "No-tail is always around."

Drew rolls his eyes. "I'm talking about Bellamy. She always seems to be around too."

"You're mouthy today."

He fishes a sucker out of his pocket and offers it to me. When I shake my head, he unwraps it and pops it in his mouth. "I was just making sure we were alone before I told you about the photographers I caught trying to get past the front gate of your property yesterday."

"Dang. They just don't know when to quit. At least they think I'm serving house arrest at my house and not here."

"I can't believe no one from the church has ratted you out yet."

"They ain't like that."

Drew pulls out his pocketknife and slices through the tape on the box. "For the right price, bet they would be."

"Nah. Surprisingly enough, Valley Church knows what integrity means." I start laying parts out on the rubber mat.

"You sound like you mean that."

"I do, man. You've been around the Men's Group and Bellamy enough to see that."

"Yeah. They alright acting." Drew tosses the empty box. "I'm out. Let me know what you want me to bring by for supper."

"Okay. Thanks."

He waves over his shoulder. "No problem."

The rest of the day flies by without me seeing Bellamy again. That's probably for the best because I'm starting to expect her in my routine. And this routine is temporary, but I keep forgetting that fact.

Bellamy storms into the shop the next day while I'm working on wiring a bike and pops me with the book. "I've been up all night because of you! And I thought the hero died!"

"Well, did he?" I set the pliers down on the workbench and wipe my hands with a clean rag.

"No!" She plops down on the couch and rubs her eyes. "I couldn't put it down. Now I know what people mean by a book hangover." She groans, sounding right miserable.

"Okay, so maybe find something else to do besides reading." I shrug, thinking that solves the problem, as my mind starts sorting through other options to distract her. "Maybe start baking... I could get behind that."

Bellamy glances up. "What do you mean by that?"

"Umm..."

"Are you intentionally trying to find me a hobby? Why?"

"I uh... So, I use fixing things as a distraction from life. I thought it'd do you good to find a distraction, too." I scratch my chin, the bristling sound saying it's time for a shave. "Are you into knitting or painting?"

She leans back and really looks at me, those gold eyes laser-focused. "You can't fix me, Lee."

"I know that, Bellamy. Only you can do that, but that's not going to stop me from trying. I just hoped the reading would be a step in the right direction, but we can find something else."

"Too late for that. I already one-clicked every one of her books. I actually considered calling in sick so I could start another one." Bellamy shakes her head, looking baffled but so beautiful that I can't take my eyes off her. "I never knew a book could capture me completely like that." She looks up and then does a double-take. "What's wrong?"

"What do you mean?" I shove my hands into the back pockets of my jeans.

"Your face... You're smiling for *real*."

"Huh?"

She stands from the couch and waves a hand toward my face. "This is the first real smile I've seen you wear."

"I'm just happy that you enjoyed the book."

"Lee Sutton, you're handsome with a scowl on your
face or a smirk, but with a genuine smile, you're
devastating." She shakes her head.

Taken aback, my lips curl up even more. "Are you
flirting with me?"

"What? No!" Bellamy starts backing up, bumping into
the coffee table in front of the couch. "This is your fault."
She points the book at me. "And this book's... it has me
thinking like a romantic..."

"Ah, Belle, you're in trouble now." I tsk and slowly
shake my head.

"Why?" Her eyes go wide as she continues in reverse
until her back is against the side door. I take it as a good
sign that she's not trying to find the doorknob.

"I don't let many people in my circle." I take a few
careful steps in her direction but keep some space between
us for her benefit. "Only my nephews, Drew, and my crew
are allowed in. It's an all-boys club. Not even my stepsister
Nichole has made it in."

Bellamy clutches the book to her chest. She's wearing
her librarian outfit today, complete with a cardigan and the
book as an accessory. And that severe bun is just begging
me to take it out and make a mess of her hair.

"Why are you telling me this?" Her voice trembles.

I release a deep sigh and steal a few more feet, drawing
me close enough to get a hint of warm scent. "Because
you've somehow gotten a foot inside the circle without me
realizing it... Seriously, Belle, once you're in I won't let
you go, so you better decide right now whether you're in or
out." My hands stay in my back pockets to keep myself in
check, but it's killing me not to reach out and cup her
flushed cheeks.

She swallows and then lets out a light cough. "Beau is
the only person to ever call me Belle."

Bellamy's reaction every time I call her that makes
perfect sense now. I place a boot on each side of her dress

shoes, getting in her space, and gaze down at her. It makes me feel bad for all of a second about calling her that before I decide to own it. "Beau was a wise man."

"He was, and he'd probably warn me not to step my other foot in your circle." Bellamy sniffs and blinks several times. "But I think it's too late."

The moment grows too heavy, the only noises are her sniffling and my heavy breaths. It lasts until I can't stand it any longer, so I take a hand out of my pocket and reach behind her until finding the doorknob. Knowing we need to pause on this line before crossing it completely, I twist the knob to set her free for now. Taking a step to the side, I hold the door open for her. When she gives me a confused look, I say, "It's not too late. Think about it."

Bellamy frowns. "How'd we end up here?" She shakes her head and hurries off.

I'm just as confused by it as Bellamy. I've sparred with this woman for four months, bickering almost daily, yet somewhere along the way we connected. I don't even know what to do with that, so I try ignoring it by focusing on the bike and work on knocking it out so I can start on my chores.

Chapter Ten

Bellamy

The season has settled into fall, leaves have changed, the air continuously holds a crispness to its quality, and the clouds have begun to hover over the mountains on a regular basis. All of this occurs even though I'm unable to pay it any attention, because my own season of life is finally changing after two years. I've been held captive in a deep mournful state, but recently that state has transformed into a confusing one.

I've watched the video once a night for the past week instead of repeatedly, and only halfway through last night before shutting it off to read. This change feels both freeing and terrifying at the same time. When I said "I do" to Beau, my intentions were a forever commitment. One that wouldn't be complete until death do us part, and that wasn't supposed to happen until Beau and I were old and gray. Coming to terms with it already being complete decades before it should, leaves me sick to my stomach.

With my eyes trained on the new day rising through the kitchen window, I take a sip of coffee. I've sipped coffee at this tiny table for over two years now, but this morning a memory wiggles loose from this action.

In a blink I'm back in our old kitchen at the bar, sitting shoulder to shoulder with Beau as we did each morning. I'm sipping coffee while he sips from a can of Sprite.

"You make no sense, Beau McCoy. Sprite doesn't even have caffeine in it."

He looked over and grinned. "I want to start my days with what makes me happy. A can of Sprite and having my lady by my side does that for me. Doesn't matter if it makes any sense... I'm happy."

Beau knew how to find happiness in the purest of forms. A can of decaffeinated pop or simply sitting with me in silence each morning made him light up like it was the grandest of gifts. He didn't live nearly long enough but, by golly, the man lived in each second while he was here.

Sighing deeply, I set the coffee cup on the table and pick up the first note from Waverly, knowing I need to deal with a few issues so I can start living again. Not doing so is like dishonoring the life my husband stood for. The envelope is creased and worn in spots from me picking it up and then putting it away several times, but today I'm resolved to face whatever is inside it. I pry the seal open and pull out a sheet of lined paper. Bracing myself, I unfold it and read the words written with an unsteady hand.

I'm sorry. So, so sorry.

Blinking and then rereading it, I let out the breath I was holding. I'm not sure what I was expecting, but one lone line was not it. Perhaps it's a good thing, because it didn't have the monumental impact on me that I expected. Relieved and a little hopeful, I slip the letter back into the envelope and place it with the others, but after a few moments of staring at it, I think of a better action. I pick it up and walk it to the trash, finally taking a step toward moving on. It may be a baby step, but I'll take it.

I place my cup in the sink and head to work. I'm there within ten minutes and quickly hop out of the truck to go tell Lee I finally read a letter. He's been on me about reading them and being done with it. He doesn't beat around the bush about things and never coddles me like everyone else. It's refreshing, even though sometimes his bluntness leaves a sting.

Before I can open the door, loud banging causes me to slow my roll. Pausing to listen, I hear him letting out a longwinded rant, complete with a few choice words weaved in. That's followed by something crashing to the floor. Yanking the door open, I stumble into a wild mess of brokenness. There's a hole in the wall where the flat screen used to be. Said flat screen is smashed to ruins on the floor, along with other unidentifiable objects.

"Lee?" I yell over his cursing. "What's wrong?"

He wheels around, red-faced and glaring. "Everything!" He shoves the workbench, tipping it over and sending out a loud clanging of tools and parts as they ricochet off the cement floor.

"Stop being a drama queen for a minute and explain to me what is actually wrong." I walk over and grab his arm when he snatches up a bike part and takes on a pitcher's stance. I place my other hand on his heaving chest. "Take a breath, Lee, and tell me."

He drops the part and runs his fingers through his blond hair. It's standing on end as if he's already attacked it several times. "Gavin is in the hospital and the judge won't let me go check on him. The a... he said unless Gavin is in critical condition, he won't permit it."

"Well, that's a good thing, right? Gavin isn't critical?" I squeeze his arm.

Lee nods before using the heels of his hands to rub his eyes. "He's dehydrated and needs a blood transfusion." His rugged voice sounds a little rougher.

It tugs at me, so I step closer and wrap my arms around his waist.

"What are you doing, Belle?" Lee asks in a gruff whisper.

"I'm holding you together. How about holding me back so it'll work better." I press my ear over his rapidly strumming heart and wait several long minutes before his solid arms encircle me. I'm considered tall for a woman, but Lee makes me feel dainty and fragile when I'm cocooned by him like this. Or he does, until his body starts trembling and he begins sniffling.

"Those boys are the reason I moved back to Tennessee... To be a male role model when their dad ditched them... And I've done nothing but screw it up..." The trembling intensifies. "What's wrong with me?" Lee sounds sincerely baffled and so, so broken.

It's evident that his own childhood issues have played a part in it, but it doesn't feel like the time to point that out. Lee doesn't really need an answer and I refuse to coddle him with meaningless, pretty words, but I do stand here in silence and hold him a little tighter.

Lee walks me backwards and around the mess littered on the floor until we reach the couch. Sitting down while wrapped in each other's arms, he buries his damp face against the side of my neck. We remain like this—Lee trembling in my arms as I comb my fingers through his hair—until his sniffles turn to heavy breaths against my neck, making me wonder if he's fallen asleep. I don't try to find out, just keep holding him.

More moments pass and then a jolt spikes through me when his lips brush against the heated skin near my ear. Perhaps I imagined it or it was simply an accident, so I ignore the affect that small touch has on me and keep holding him tightly. I try to focus on soothing him, but my entire body freezes when his lips press down in several spots. There's no denying he's kissing my neck deliberately. All I can do is sit rigidly as the warmth of that contact both frightens me as well as sparks something deep inside that I've not felt in a very long time.

Suddenly, Lee freezes for a split second too, then jumps off the couch. "I'm sorry." He backs away a few steps and rubs his jaw, then waves around at the trashed garage. "I didn't mean to scare you and then... I'm sorry."

My fingertips press against the damp spot on my neck as I stare up at him. "I'm not scared of you... I'm scared of how you make me feel." I confess this to put him at ease, but his expression says I did anything but.

"Bellamy, I'm warning you..." Lee takes a giant step in my direction like he's ready to pounce, but I get up and head to the door.

"Just take the day off and get yourself together. I'll let Chase know." I hurry out, not waiting for a reply, and head straight into Chase's office.

I pause at the cracked door, just out of view, and try to get my erratic heartrate under control. Breathing in and out, I smooth my sweaty palms down the side of my dress pants and then knock on the door.

"Good morning," Chase mumbles while peering down at his Bible through his glasses.

I scoot inside and stand before Chase's desk. "Lee isn't feeling well today. I told him to take the day off."

Chase looks up. "Okay. Does he need a doctor?"

"No. Nothing like that." I wave his concerns off. "Gavin is in the hospital and the judge won't allow Lee to go visit... He's distraught." I plop in the chair in front of the desk. "Is there anything we can do about that?"

Chase sighs and leans back in his chair. "Not really. Lee being here is a giant favor in itself. I don't think we have any room to be asking for anything more. I can go visit Gavin and give Lee an update. Do you know how the boy is doing?"

"Lee says he's dehydrated and needs another blood transfusion, but it's not critical."

"Well, that's good news, right?"

I scrub my hands down my face. "That's what I tried to tell him, but he's still pretty upset."

"I see you've taken your rings off."

I drop my hands with guilt washing over me. "I..."

Chase raises his palms. "It's a good thing, Bellamy. Two and a half years... It's time." His hazel eyes turn glassy but his smile is genuine with a hint of pride.

I nod and glance out the window, trying to push my thoughts in another direction before the blubbering can begin. "I have a meeting with the program committee, but after that, if it's alright with you, I'd like to go check on Gavin."

"I think that's a great idea." Chase blinks the heaviness away from his eyes and picks up his Bible. "Listen to this verse from Isaiah I'm studying... 'Whether you turn to the right or to the left, your ears will hear a voice behind you, saying, "This is the way; walk in it."'"

"Good verse," I comment, rising to my feet.

"It is. Keep listening, Bellamy. Allow Him to lead you to whatever He has planned. Don't let grief and fear hold you back from receiving the blessings God has in store for you, my friend."

My throat thickens and my nose begins to sting. I want to hug my brother-in-law at the same time an urge to pop him crosses my mind. Almost twenty years my senior, Chase has always been more of a father figure and a great shepherd. His words have always been such an important guide. Even when they hurt. Even when they are spot-on and I want to ignore them.

As it is, all I can do is nod and rush out the door.

Chapter Eleven

Lee

The long-taught lesson of actions having consequences has been one that's nagged me from a young age. Once, I convinced Tommy the brightly wrapped chocolate squares I found in our grandma's medicine cabinet were candy for his taking. Tommy was a pudgy kid and loved sweets, so it wasn't surprising when he took me up on it. He traded me some packs of gum, because that was my weakness, for the chocolate and we both thought we'd won a pot of gold. Hours later, the only pot we had privy to was the toilet. I'd tricked him with laxatives in the deceptive form of chocolate, and my brother played the same trick on me with Feen-a-mint laxative gum. Sadly, that pot was at the local pizza joint where our parents had taken us for supper. We spent a long time in that public restroom, Tommy in one stall while I occupied the other. All the while, the owner stood outside the door, begging our parents to take us home. Momma said she would if she could, but, well, our actions had some pretty dire consequences. Needless to say, we closed the Pizza Pub down that night and our stupid pranks robbed us of pizza buffet heaven. I also lost my taste for chewing gum.

Later that night, I had to go to the emergency room due to dehydration. Tommy stood by my hospital bed, crying and asking me to forgive him. I didn't get it, because I pulled the same prank on him and never felt the need to apologize. But that was Tommy. He had a heart, and I'm fairly certain it was made mostly of gold. I was beyond baffled when, within months, our roles would be reversed with me standing by Tommy's hospital bed. Why did Tommy have the brain tumor and not me? He was good. I was not. I deserved it. He did not. I never figured out why he had to endure the consequence of cancer when I got off scot-free.

I hate consequences.

Sitting in the garage, fuming, I know there's no one to blame for the consequence of me being stuck here but myself. I assess the broken mess left in the wake of my rage this morning, looking for something I may be able to piece back together. The TV is beyond repair, but the remote looks promising. Releasing a huff, I bend down to pick the pieces up as the phone starts going off.

Straightening, I glance at it on the coffee table and see it's a facetime request from Bellamy. I hit accept and settle against the cushions of the couch while watching her face fill the screen. "Hey, beautiful."

"Umm... Hi." Bellamy glances to the left of the screen. "I have someone very important who wants to talk to you." She disappears and a tiled floor fills the screen before moving around and settling on a precious sight.

"Uncle Lee," Gavin says. His voice is weak but he's grinning.

Clearing the tightness from my throat, I reply, "Hey, kid. How you feeling?" I bite my bottom lip to stop it from wobbling. Man, it's killing me that I can't go to him.

"Not so good." He frowns.

"What's not good?" I raise the phone a little higher, trying to get a better look at him.

"I ain't eating, so they're talking about putting in a tube." He wrinkles his nose and it makes my gut hurt when remembering him having to deal with a feeding tube about a year ago.

I scan the garage and stop on the covered bike. "Hey, guess what bike I have to wire."

"I don't know." Gavin's interest is nonexistent, so I get off the couch and move over to pull the cover off.

"Check this out," I say and flip the screen around to show off the Ironman themed chopper, which happens to be this kid's favorite Marvel superhero.

"Whoa…" His whoa is a weak whoa, but it's a whoa all the same.

"Yeah. It's gotta go to Hollywood, but I need you to copilot the test drive before I can okay it to be shipped."

There's a spark in his brown eyes, but it doesn't last long. "I wish you could come get me now."

"Me too, buddy. Me too." I maneuver around the junk scattered on the floor and plop down on the couch. No-tail joins me and puts his nosy nose to the phone screen, eliciting a faint giggle from Gavin. "This spoiled, fat cat misses you… Say, how about you promise to do everything the doctors and nurses tell you to do, and I promise to push back the bike shipment until you're strong enough to ride it with me."

"For real? They'd let you do that?"

I scoff. "I'm the boss, ain't I?"

Gavin smiles at that. "You said the other day that Ms. Bellamy thinks she's the boss."

I hear Bellamy clearing her throat in the background and Nichole snickering. "Women…" I roll my eyes and play it off. "How about telling me what you feel like eating and let the boss man handle that, too."

His bony shoulder hitches up. "Nothing tastes good."

"Nothing?"

He shakes his head, crooking the oxygen tube. I'm about to tell him to straighten it when Nichole's hand appears and takes care of it.

"Pizza?"

"No."

"Happy meal?"

"I'm eleven."

"So."

"No."

"Bucket of chicken?"

"No."

"Chinese? I could go for some of that."

"Hmm… What about that place that cooks it in front of you? Remember you took us there one time. I like the fried rice. Is that Chinese?" Gavin doesn't sound very convincing but at least he's suggested something.

"Japanese. That's good stuff too. Now, how about a smoothie from that fancy place y'all like in town? Strawberry?"

"I guess…"

"We're talking *Ironman* here, buddy. You gotta man up and do this, so this is your chance to get anything you want to get it done."

"Okay." Gavin lets out a yawn.

"Okay," I echo. "I'm going to get Drew on picking up the food and delivering it to you. He'll have a surprise for you too, but you gotta drink the smoothie and eat to get it."

"What surprise?"

"You gotta eat to find out." I give him a pointed look. "I love you, kid. How about putting Bellamy on?"

"Love you, Uncle Lee." Gavin disappears and Bellamy comes back into view.

"Yes, boss?" She glares but it has too much sass to be serious.

"Babe, you just stepped the other foot in the circle. You get that, right?"

"Umm… I think so." Her eyes move away from me as color rises in her cheeks.

With too many ears listening, I let it go for now and focus on what I can do for Gavin. "I need to get the food ordered. You gonna stick around there for a while?" I ask and she nods. "That means a lot. Thank you."

I hang up and shoot a text to Drew, instructing him to pick up food, a smoothie, and a new gaming system with every racing game he can find. Then tell him he's to hang out with Gavin and play video games with him for a few hours each day until the kid gets to come home. He replies with a thumbs-up and it makes me feel good to know he'll handle it. The punk is loyal, and it makes me thankful he tried stealing my bike way back when.

Restless, I clean up the mess I made in the garage and then go find Chase. I hit my knuckles against his door and he calls for me to come in. I find him where he is most days, behind his desk studying his Bible with a notepad and pen beside it.

"What needs to be done today?" I ask, staying beside the door even though he motions for me to come in.

"I'm sorry about Gavin. I've added him to our prayer chain. You can take a personal day, Lee. I understand." Chase meets my eyes over the top of his glasses.

"I can't sit still. It's best to keep busy."

Chase nods. "I can call the nursery and have them deliver the mulch for the flowerbeds. Sound good?"

I'm not sure why he gives me a choice when I certainly don't deserve it. "What company? I can call them so you can keep at what you're doing." I tip my head toward his Bible.

"If you're sure…" Chase jots down something on a sticky note and holds it out toward me. "They already have the order ready and were waiting for me to let them know when to bring it over."

I take a few steps inside, grab the note, and make a one-eighty back out the door. "I'm on it."

Within the hour, a delivery truck is backing up and dumping a mound of river rocks off to the side of the church, near the flowerbeds. After I sign the invoice and credit card slip, I make quick work of clearing and lining the beds with the roll of barrier material. With a pair of gloves on and a shovel in hand, I'm about to start filling a wheelbarrow when Chase hustles toward me with his dress shoes clapping against the sidewalk.

"The order is wrong. It's supposed to be wood mulch."

"Yeah." I dig the shovel in and dump a scoop into the wheelbarrow. "I changed it."

"Why?" Chase keeps hovering but I keep scooping, needing to work the frustration out of my system before I lose it.

"River rock looks better and you'll never have to replace it. Makes more sense." I grunt, digging the shovel in for a bigger scoop.

"Lee, you can't keep purchasing things. Give me the invoice so we can reimburse you."

"Nah, man. Least I can do with y'all having to put up with me."

"It's not been a burden having you here, I hope you know."

I glance up and watch him grab a smooth stone and turn it in his hands. "You've been too welcoming. Too kind. I don't get it." I use the back of my glove to catch a drop of perspiration about to escape into my eye. Even though it's cold out, I've worked up a mean sweat. "Just... Let's just drop it, okay?"

"Okay. Stop by my office when you're done." Chase places the rock back into the wheelbarrow and walks away.

I watch him go, wondering why he's always so agreeable about everything. Shaking my head, I lose myself in manual labor until my back and shoulder muscles are on fire, the rock pile is gone, and the sun is setting. Satisfied with the immaculate landscaping, I put the tools away and go check in with Chase. I peek my head around the door with the plan of telling him I'm done before heading to the waterfall for a much-needed shower, but he's on the phone and gestures for me to wait a minute.

A wall of plaques and framed certificates catch my eye, so I wander over and can't help but be impressed by what they proclaim. Masters in Psychology, a theology degree, and a certificate naming Chase McCoy as a Professional Psychiatrist.

When I hear Chase hang up the phone, I turn to him and hitch a thumb to the framed credentials. "You're legit. All this time I thought people came in here for prayer and scripture."

"That's part of it." Chase looks over my shoulder where his credentials are displayed.

"You counsel Neena and Asher Reid," I state.

"I'm not at liberty to say." Chase takes his readers off and places them on top of an open agenda book. His answer earns him some more respect in my book.

"So if, say, we talk about stuff in here, you won't be at liberty to discuss that with anyone else either?"

"Nope. It stays in here, between us and God."

I take a step over to a book shelf and scan the pictures until stopping on one of Chase with his arm around the shoulders of a younger guy who resembles him, the two of them standing in front of a small building. "This Beau?" I already know it's him because it's the same guy from the wedding picture in Bellamy's office.

"Yes. That was taken on a mission trip to Guatemala. We helped to build the church behind us in the picture. Beau always had a heart for mission."

"I lost a younger brother, too," I admit, surprising myself with the words.

"How old was he?"

"Nine. He had cancer." Feeling drained suddenly, I walk over and have a seat in front of Chase's desk.

"I looked over your record and noticed the charges only started in the last few years. What happened to cause this?"

"I moved my business back here to be closer to family. I really wanted to give it a shot to get close to them, and it was going great. I loved having my nephews hanging out at my shop getting into junk and horsing around. They remind me a lot of me and Tommy. Then my nephew Gavin started getting sickly."

"But he doesn't have cancer, correct?"

"He has an autoimmune disorder and the poor kid stays anemic."

"Bet that brought back some bad memories." Chase steeples his fingers and waits out my silence.

The reel of all the bad plays out in my mind—Tommy withering from the ruthless disease, Tommy in a casket, Momma curled in a ball in bed, Pop stumbling around the living room blistered out of his mind, Momma driving away, Pop driving away.

"Lee?"

I look up, blinking several times. "It felt like I was thrown right back into the situation with what happened with Tommy. I couldn't deal, so I started spiraling." Taking a shaky breath, I ask, "How'd you deal with your brother being killed?"

Chase's forehead puckers as he drops his hands and pinches the bridge of his nose. "Honestly, it still hurts, but through a lot prayer, seeking God in the darker times, and leaning on my family, I've managed the grief."

I can't help but snort out a humorless laugh.

"What?"

"Nothing." I go to stand, not wanting to have a religious talk.

"You believe in God, right?"

"Yeah, man. No way can you live in this world and not believe there's a creator greater than us." I point out the window where the mountains loom in the short distance.

"Then what's the problem?"

I grip the back of the chair until my fingers ache. "Who's supposed to love you unconditionally?"

"God—"

"Besides him."

"Your parents."

"Yeah, well, mine didn't. After my brother died, they forgot about me. Both walked away. My parents didn't care enough to be there for me, so why should I believe I'm good enough for our Creator to want to be there for me?"

"Lee, I'm sorry about how your parents treated you." Chase's phone goes off, and he mutters an apology but surprises me by shutting it off instead of answering it. After he places it in his desk drawer, he focuses back on me. "Sometimes people don't know how to handle grief and go about dealing with it the wrong way."

I glance over my shoulder toward the door. "Don't make excuses for them."

"I'm not talking about them. I'm talking about you," Chase says, making me snap my attention back around. He waves a hand at me. "You obviously don't know how to handle your grief over Gavin being sick, so you turned to self-destruction... Do you worry about him blaming himself for your transgressions?"

"Why would he? That's ridiculous. It's all on me." I pound my fist against the back of the chair, ready to scream.

"You don't think Gavin ever wonders if he isn't good enough for you to keep your act straight? That him being sick has caused you to get into trouble?"

Right then I know what he's doing and I hate it. Chase just forced me to take the blinders off and realize I'm repeating the history of my parents and quite possibly setting Gavin on a path to do the same. The revelation has me plopping into the chair. "I'm no better than my parents..."

"I don't know your parents, but I have a feeling they never intended for their pain to bleed all over you any more than you meant for it to bleed all over your nephews." Chase moves around his desk and takes the seat beside me. "I'm not excusing your parents' or your behavior. But what I'm hoping is for you to realize the wrong in it and make a better choice for you and your family's sake."

We just sit here, listening to three cycles of the heating system before he speaks again. "Fact of life is people will always let you down if you put your faith completely in them."

I stop studying the irregular pattern of the carpet and look over at him. "Have people let you down?"

"*I've* let people down." Chase taps his chest and glances at the shelf holding the pictures. "I asked Beau to stay an extra day at the conference in Nashville so I could get back home to see my grandson's T-ball game. If I hadn't been selfish and asked Beau to stay to cover one of my sessions, then he wouldn't have been on the road that night. I let my brother down."

Two more cycles of the heater edge by while I take in what he said and he sits there waiting with an endless supply of patience. The more I think about it, the more foolish I feel. "What do ya reckon I need to do?"

"You need to realize our God is greater than your worst. There's no way I would be able to live with Beau's death had I not put my faith completely in God and asked him to help me overcome my guilt and grief." Chase reaches over and grasps my shoulder. "Lee, it didn't happen right away. Not because God couldn't handle it, but because I wouldn't give it completely over to him. And how mighty God is that he patiently waited for me to do so. If you've not asked him to be first and foremost in your life, I encourage you to consider beginning there."

I nod, still coming to terms with all the truths this man just dished out to me. It's so clear and makes so much sense that I'm completely baffled by it. I'm a detail guy, and now that these details are before me, there's no ignoring them. It's time to sort it out and do something with them.

"Do you mind if I pray with you before you go?"

I clear my throat and mumble, "I guess not."

With his hand remaining on my shoulder, Chase stuns me by starting his prayer by thanking God for me. *Me.* Then he asks for Gavin's healing and then my family's healing and concludes with the same request for me. He says amen and releases my shoulder, so I take that as my cue to leave.

At the door, I turn around and say, "You're a standup guy, preacher."

Chase straightens his tie and smooths the sleeves of his dress shirt. "I do my best." He grins.

The thing about Chase McCoy is you can't help but like the guy. He's like the older, slightly nerdy buddy who everyone can count on and enjoys having around. I never thought I'd actually want to hang out with a preacher man, but I'm starting to realize I've been wrong in my thinking about a lot of things.

Chapter Twelve

Bellamy

Something's happened to Lee since Gavin's hospital stay a few weeks ago. Thankfully, Gavin is home and on the mend and was able to test ride the Ironman bike around the church parking lot. I thought Lee's odd mood was just over being emotional about Gavin, but it's not like he's upset or angry. He seems more grounded at the same time he seems quite distracted. Lee also went from dodging church services to attending them all, which would make one think he's feeling more social, except that he's grown a good bit quieter. I'm not sure what to think about it, but I'm too distracted by my own case to figure his out.

I've read all twenty-six letters, each one starting with the same line: *I'm sorry. So, so sorry.* The lines proceeding are filled with Waverly's regrets, but never an excuse for what he did.

I reread the last line of the last letter. *I wish it were me who died and not your husband. It should have been me.*

With a heavy heart, I toss number twenty-six in the trash, knowing more needs to be done than reading and discarding this man's confessions. I just don't know if I'm strong enough.

I leave the letter in the garbage with hopes some of my hatred for the man remains there as well. Thanksgiving is coming up quickly, and a lot of events at the church are just on the horizon. Looking over the calendar in my phone, I decide to head on to work and start tackling some of the details.

The Men's Group is meeting this morning so it's no surprise to see a few early birds have already arrived. After stewing over Waverly's letters and the mixed emotions they have stirred, I'm not feeling very social, so I toss a wave in their direction and beeline to my office to stay hunkered behind the desk until midmorning. The only pause in work is to snag a cup of coffee and to open my window to allow the sweet mountain air in.

Halfway through an email, the chattering sound of a bunch of excited men slips through the window. Glancing that way, I see Lee pushing that monster of a bike out of the garage as the older men gather around him. His stupid reminder, as he called it, is finally fixed, and I have to admit it's quite impressive.

Watching him build bikes over the last few months, I've come to the conclusion that bike building is an artform. It's amazing to witness him take a raw piece of metal and sculpt it into a functioning part of the motorcycle. His eye for detail is nothing short of a gift. The bike being ogled outside right now is a case in point. It looked like a piece of mangled scrap metal the first time I laid eyes on it, but today it's showcase worthy. A vintage teal and cream paintjob, accented with chrome and buttery-brown leather. Lee refers to it as a chopper, but I consider it one sleek beast.

I scoot over to the window to get a better view of what they are up to.

Lee pulls out a helmet and hands it to Harvey. "First rule. Anyone riding with me has to wear a helmet."

"Even in the parking lot?" Harvey asks, slipping his cap off and replacing it with the helmet.

"Even in a parking lot." Lee adjusts the strap underneath Harvey's chin, and then points to the chrome piece on the back of the seat. "Use the sissy bar to help get on."

Harvey scoffs. "I ain't a sissy."

Lee shrugs his wide shoulders, looking like a giant compared to Harvey. "I can pick you up and sit you on the bike and that'll definitely make you look like a sissy."

Harvey reaches for the sissy bar without further complaint. Poor fellow tries his best to swing his leg over the giant bike, but Lee finally has to give him a boost.

"I got a bad shoulder, Lee, so I'm gonna have to hold on to you. That make me a sissy?"

"No, sir. That makes you old." Lee pretends to punch him in the shoulder. "But that also makes you smart." With no effort or grunting like Harvey, Lee simply lifts his leg over the bike and has a seat in one fluid motion.

Lee begins walking the bike backwards. He glances up and catches me watching. I'm rewarded with one of his genuine smiles and a quick wink before he turns his attention to the group of men.

"If y'all get me in trouble with the boss lady for slacking off with you instead of polishing pews, you're taking the blame."

"We are to blame," Jeb quickly admits.

Lee looks my way again. "As long as it's been noted."

"We been begging for two weeks for this. It's cruel to deny men with one foot in the grave what they ask for. Seems like this should be counted as community service hours," Clarence adds.

"Nah. Hanging out with you guys is a blast. It's gotta be against the rules for a prisoner to have such a good time."

The men laugh and then suddenly it's drowned out by the massive roar of the bike's engine. It's not only heard but felt, the windowpanes rattling from the vibration. It's so powerful, goose bumps break out along my arms, and I can't help but grin when I notice each man's lips are formed in an awed O shape with eyes wide.

No doubt about it, Lee Sutton is their Santa Claus and he just came to town.

For the next hour, my ears ring as the loud beast makes lap after lap until each of the men have had a turn. Then they give commentary on what they think about the bike, all of which is positive and quite boyish. I stay at my desk, grinning and snickering to myself while listening to them until someone clears their throat near my window.

Jolting in my chair, I look up and find Lee leaning in. "You scared me," I scold him.

"Sorry, but it's time for the boss's turn."

"Turn for what?" I stand up and walk over to the window and notice the Men's Group standing just a few feet behind Lee. "Hello, guys."

"Get yourself out here," Clarence speaks up and waves an arm at the bike like he's a gameshow host.

"Oh no. I don't think so." I shake my head, but Lee leans in and pulls me right out the window with little effort. "Hey!"

"You know you want to, so stop playing us." Lee sets me down, gathers my hand in his, and in only a few strides has us positioned by the monstrous bike. He gently places the helmet on my head. Too gentle for such a rugged man, but he manages it with graceful finesse. He takes his time lining up the chin strap and snapping it into place, sending wave after wave of tingles to dance along my neck and shoulders. The smile pulling at one side of his lips indicates Lee knows what he's doing to me, but thankfully he doesn't tease me about it.

I quickly climb on the bike, not giving Lee the opportunity to help me like he did the other men. Once I'm settled, I chance a glance at him and notice him considering me with much thought. I narrow my eyes and incline my head to the side. He takes the hint and settles himself in front of me. I'm hyperaware of each point of contact—my knees pressing his thighs, my chest grazing his back, his fingertips briefly squeezing my calf as he positions my leg in a safer spot...

I'm so entranced by this that the sudden growl of the engine makes me flinch in such a spastic manner, I'm surprised I didn't fall off the bike. This time his fingertips squeeze my knee for assurance. Worried the men are noticing me unravel by this man's innocent touches, I cut my eyes in their direction and only find them smiling. Each one either gives me a thumbs-up or an encouraging wave as they begin shuffling toward the fellowship hall.

Once we're alone, Lee turns his head and leans back, looking as if he's going in for a kiss, but talks over the roar of the engine instead. "Wrap your arms around my waist and hold on!"

I shake my head, which sends one of his thick eyebrows to arch. "I can balance on my own," I yell.

Now Lee shakes his head and leans toward me even more until his back is firmly pressed against me. "Yeah. You could, but the ride will be more enjoyable if you hold on and we balance together. It's tiresome to do it on your own." There's no missing the double meaning to his words or the sincere look he gives me.

Blinking a few times, I stare into those deep-blue eyes and notice something new peeking out from the starbursts. It's a twinkle of hope starting to overtake the shadows of despair. A wobbly smile pulls my lips upward as I nod my head once.

Lee accepts my permission, reaching for my hands and then wrapping my arms around his lean waist. "Please don't let go, Belle." He gently squeezes my hands for emphasis before leaning away and directing his focus on easing the bike around the parking lot.

The sun is bright and warm enough to combat the chill in the air, and Lee's broad shoulders protect me from the wind. A few laps in, I shake off the tension keeping my body rigid and give in to the natural flow our bodies take with each turn and curve the bike makes. It's a fluid dance, reminding me of how well life itself can move from one place in time to another with the right guidance and support. It's also an unpleasant reminder of how unbalanced my life has become in the last few years, with me trying to right it on my own.

As we make another lap, I wish Lee could race out of the parking lot and take me away from everything. It's on the tip of my tongue to suggest this until I look down and catch the ankle monitor peeping out at the edge of his pants leg. I swallow the lump in my throat, realizing there will be no true balance to my life until I take care of some past-due business, no matter how painful it's going to be.

Giving in, I place my cheek against the back of his shoulder and slide my hands into the warmth of his hoodie pockets. I pretend for the remainder of the ride we're both free and living a balanced life where no hurts can reach us from our perch on the bike. Lee is so solid and soothing that I almost forget.

****

Mountains surround the three-story gray-bricked building centered in the middle of a well-maintained plot of land. It almost feels inviting. The only elements that would induce a visitor to pause are the high-voltage fence lining the property and the sign declaring it to be Lone Valley Correctional Facility.

I pull the truck up to the fence, roll the window down, and push the intercom button before my nerves send me in the other direction. It's time to face what's waiting behind those gray walls.

After stating who I am and what my business is here, I'm instructed to pull up to the visitor parking and enter the main entrance. The tone is robotic, and I mime my inner instructions in much the same fashion.

Just keep moving forward. Don't think, just do.
Turn the engine off.

Get out of the truck.
Enter through the glass door.
Walk through the metal detector.
Don't fall apart.

Decision after decision. Outwardly, they are basic, but they're leading me to another decision that makes every inch of my body vibrate in an overwhelming ache of grief and anger. Tamping it down and focusing on working air into my lungs, I follow the guard down a corridor. Each step taps an SOS on the shiny tiled floor. Words are spoken to me, but the roar residing in my ears drowns them out. All I know is I end up in a room with a long row of sections designed to look like cubicles. Each has a chair mirroring one on the other side of the partition.

"Have a seat." The guard points to the last one on the right even though the entire place is vacant.

The quietness of the room presses down on me until the clicking of a door on the other side alerts me to the fact that my time alone is about to end. The other side of this cubicle is about to hold the object of my misery. And just like that, he appears, and my first impression is to notice how pathetic he looks.

Sallow skin, puffy from little rest. Eyes reddened and lined with deep wrinkles. Nothing more than a shadow of a man, wispy in height and weight. It's mindboggling that such a tiny, unimpressive human had the power to take my husband's life.

We do nothing more than stare, him off into space and me at him, and the more I study Carl Waverly, the more I see a harsh burden in his features. The trembling of his bottom lip. The straining bob of his neck each time he tries to swallow. The pain in his eyes each time he tries and fails to make eye contact with me. Minutes tick by while I conclude that the word *pathetic* may not be the right term. *Pitiful* may be more accurate, but it seems too kind of a word for him.

"I'm sorry—"

I throw my hand up and slowly shake my head to hush his frail voice. "No... No more apologies. You stated that in all twenty-six letters." My composure begins to slip, so I pause to clear my throat. "Today, I want you to tell me what led up to you killing my husband."

Another long stretch of uncomfortable silence ensues after I choke on the last part of my demand. Each time Waverly's throat bobs my own constricts. I try to steel myself, with little success, but it doesn't matter. He's falling apart just as rapidly.

"I drunk too much—"

My hand shoots up again. "No! I want the full story. You owe Beau as much."

Waverly nods his head and rubs a hand through his mousy brown hair. It's as dull as his complexion. "My wife and I... Well, we were going through a rough patch... Look, I don't want to make an excuse for my actions."

"I'm not asking for an excuse. I need an explanation as to what led you to make such a devastating choice."

He takes a deep breath, his eyes continuing to skirt my gaze. "Everything just kept falling apart..." His shoulders droop even further, making the baggy gray jumpsuit look like it's swallowing him.

"Go on," I insist when he hushes.

Waverly places his shackled hands on top of the table and starts picking at his nails. I'm surprised to see the anger of his expression.

"I'm sorry. Is this conversation inconveniencing you? Did I interrupt your TV time to ask why you killed my husband?" I ball my fists until my nails bite into my palms.

"I'm nothing but a failure," he whispers through gritted teeth. Sniffing, he raises his eyes but stalls on my nose. "The more I tried to make things better, the worse I made them... After years of trying to conceive, we found out I was the reason we couldn't have children. I thought I could make that up to my wife, if we had more money, so I took our savings and invested it. No surprise, I ended up losing it all. I took a chance at work with bringing in a new client and it blew up in my face. Things just kept piling up on top of me, so then that day..." He takes a shaky breath. "I lost my job and just couldn't face my wife with one more failure. It was me who was supposed to die that day. I failed at that, too."

"What do you mean?" I manage to say in a calmer tone, mindful of the guard who has moved closer behind Waverly.

"I was pretty sure they were going to fire me, and I was just too tired to fight anymore. Before I left for work that morning, I loaded my handgun and put it in the glovebox of my car. After they told me to pack my belongings, I walked out of the conference room and straight out the doors. The idea to grab the gun and end it right there on the steps of the company building felt kinda fitting." Waverly lets out a sullen laugh that ends in a frail sob. "Except I was too much of a coward to go through with it." He raises his hands, causing the chains binding his wrists to jangle, and slaps an escaped tear away.

"And?" I motion for him to continue.

"And so I stopped at a bar to drink myself into going through with it. I thought after a few drinks, I would at least be brave enough to end it in the parking lot behind the bar. But then after too many drinks, I decided to head out of town and find a secluded spot to do it... I got behind the wheel of my car with all intentions of killing myself, not your husband... The biggest failure of my life."

I watch him fall apart. The guttural sobs mimic my own pain, but for some reason, not a tear will form in my eyes. Maybe it's God's way of making sure I have a clear view of this man's brokenness. It doesn't soften me toward him, yet there is a new understanding I didn't have before walking into this prison.

When he quietens, I say, "I want to forgive you, but I honestly don't think it's going to be today."

"I don't deserve it."

"No, you most certainly don't, but you need it..." I stutter out a heavy sigh. "We both do." Admitting this hurts, but it's a hurt that needs to come to the surface and do its worst damage before we can even begin to think about healing. "May I come back another time?"

"If you want, yes." Waverly finally meets my eyes, and what I see is absolute defeat. There isn't even a trace of hope to be found. His eyes are a faded blue, but they remind me so much of another set that has held the same reflection of remorse.

I can't take any more for the day, so I simply rise from the chair and walk out of the room without another word.

On the drive home, I switch off the radio and replay what just happened over and over until I pull into my driveway. I put the truck in park and stare at my front porch while coming to two devastating conclusions.

Waverly's soul is in desperate peril.

Not forgiving him is just as reckless as what he did.

Beau would have done something to reach out to Waverly, but what on earth could I possibly do? When no answers clarify, I exit the truck and head inside.

With my energy and appetite zapped, I go straight to my room and climb into bed without bothering to change. I hunker down underneath the quilt to hide from what God is nudging me to do, but it finds me in the dark and slams into me like a tsunami. Forgiveness is a difficult gift to give. Until I decide to grant that to Waverly, I fear I'm holding myself prisoner right along with that man's soul.

Chapter Thirteen

Lee

For one minute life was feeling pretty right—riding around on my bike with an amazing woman clinging to my back. It felt like she belonged to me. That long minute lasted only until the bike started running low on fuel. As soon as I parked the bike by the garage, the spell of everything feeling pretty right evaporated. That amazing woman who had been clinging to me dropped her hold and hopped off the bike like it was the last place she wanted to be. She apologized—for what I don't know—before running off. That was five days ago, and every minute since then has felt pretty wrong.

It's the first time since I claimed a spot on this church's back pew that Bellamy isn't beside me in her spot. During the song special, I slip my phone out of my jacket and send her a text.

Are you okay?

It goes unanswered throughout the entire song. Chase takes his place behind the pulpit. I start to put the phone away, but it vibrates.

I will be.

No reply other than that and it's vague enough to raise my hackles. I send one more text, this one to Drew to meet me here in an hour, and put the phone away to focus on Chase. I've never been one to take kindly to someone yelling and pointing at me with disdain painted on their face, demanding it's their way or no way. Pastor Chase McCoy is the opposite of that. I like the guy's style of preaching. It's more of a conversation with us that's infused with a lot of wisdom and it makes me more inclined to want to apply that wisdom to my screwed-up life.

Even though Bellamy is heavy on my mind, I easily get pulled into the message about the rich young man refusing to give all of his earthly possessions away to the poor so he can enter heaven.

"I'm not saying to do without a decent roof over your head or a nice vehicle and neither is Jesus. But his message here is for us to remember to desire a heavenly hope that is everlasting and not earthly treasures that won't last." Chase looks long and hard at me, and I know before he speaks it's going to be about me, for me, or both.

He paces a moment and then looks at me again. "I have a friend who can make art from plain ole metal. I'm talking spectacular art that blows my mind." He makes another pass along the stage. "But you can ask my friend and he can attest that no matter how much time and energy he puts into fashioning his art, it can be destroyed. Something as strong and durable as metal can still be bent and twisted and tarnished to the point it's weakened and unusable. My friend can put all of his focus and time into his craft, but it's temporary no matter how beautiful or spectacular. And just as the rich young man, if my friend doesn't seek the everlasting beauty and splendor that only our heavenly Father can provide, then his happiness will always be temporary."

Several people murmur agreements as Chase paces some more.

"How much greater could my artist friend's earthly treasures be if he'd dedicate it all to Jesus? I'm talking about his focus, not his dollars. I'm talking about each time he finishes another piece of art, my friend gazes at it, knowing it's a gift from God that he can create the amazing way he creates. And then sharing that understanding with the world."

I find myself nodding my head at him. Dude should be a salesman, because the way he offers God's word is like a gift of gold served on a silver platter lined with diamonds. And just like that, I want to figure out how to transform Sutton Custom Bikes from showcasing the disaster that is me to reflecting something more positive. I'm sick of all the negative surrounding my life. It's suffocating.

Sitting here on a pew by myself, thinking about how impressed I am with the way Chase presents himself, my stomach turns sour at the realization of how poorly I present myself to others. Looks of disgust over the last few years, and more recently from Bellamy, force me to acknowledge that those grimaces are entirely my fault. The package I've presented is an arrogant, selfish jerk. Sure, I've used that as a deflecting device, but at what cost?

As the invitational hymn begins, shame sends my neck and face up in flames and has me slinking out the back of the church, fleeing like the convict I am.

By the time Drew arrives, I've put in such a rigorous workout that the sweat has completely hidden the tears.

Drew eyes me as he leans down to pet No-tail. "Dude, what's wrong with you?"

Or so I thought...

"Nothing." I pick up a towel and mop my face hard enough to make it burn. "Nothing's wrong with me, but something is up with Bellamy."

Drew straightens. "What's wrong with her?"

"I don't know. She's been a no-show at work since Tuesday and didn't come to church today, so I need you to go check on her."

He scratches his cheek. "Where she live?"

"Well, considering I've never been invited over, I don't know!" I throw my hands up and growl.

"No need for the attitude. And how the heck am I supposed to figure it out? Call up Sherlock Holmes?" He throws attitude back to me. I deserve it but I'm too frustrated to accept it, so all I do is point at the way he moseyed his punk-self in here. He doesn't budge.

"Never mind. I'll do it myself," I mumble, pushing past him.

Drew grabs my shoulder. "Whoa, man. You know you can't do that."

I yank out of his grip. "I don't care. Something's wrong."

"I'll go find her. Just..." He huffs. "You have any clue where I should start looking?"

"She leaves out to the right each day and says she lives ten minutes down the road. Head that way and look for her truck."

"And what exactly do you want me to do when I find it?"

"Good question..." I scan the garage, having no clue, but then my gaze lands on the answer. I scoop up No-tail and hand him to Drew. "Ask her to bring the cat home to me."

Drew gives me a blank stare as No-tail bats his beard. It'd be funny if my mood was better. "That's so lame."

Yes, it's lame but what other choice do I have? I cross my arms and tick my chin up. "Do it anyway."

Eyeing me, Drew starts walking backwards. "Something else is wrong with you. Been eating at you for a while now. Think it's time to be dealt with." He's out the door, which saves me from having to reply.

Even though I'm spent from the workout, my mind is restless, so I gather some tools and head over to the shed to take the lawnmower apart. It's a piece of crap and keeps choking off when I use it. Hunkered down in the dingy building, surrounded by the odors of gas fumes and decay, I have the deck torn down in no time. My phone goes off as I'm about to start on the engine. I press my blackened fingers to the screen to pull up the text from Drew.

Found her. Wouldn't let me in, but took the cat. No visible sign of damage except for her hair. It needs a brush. I'm heading home.

I stand up and roll my neck, feeling a little better than an hour ago. I leave the mower for another day and go gather supplies for a shower and a change of clothes. It's getting close to the point of being too cold to pull off waterfall showers, but today I'll take the frigid numbness it'll offer.

Stripping at the edge of the water and fishing the bottles of shampoo and body wash from the bag, I don't give my mind time to talk my body out of this decision. Just plunge into the icy pelts without fighting against the instant stinging pain the water delivers. I make quick work of washing my hair and then work up a thick lather to rid my skin of the dried sweat and grime. I hold my breath and step back into the spray of the waterfall to wash it off. Even though my feet are completely numb, I chance one more washing. As I'm rinsing off a gasp reaches me.

Opening my eyes, I find Bellamy standing on the shore, hands on her hips with her mouth hanging open.

She blinks several times, but her eyes stay fastened to me. "Goodness sake, Lee! What are you doing?"

"What's it look like I'm doing?" I flick my fingers through my hair to finish rinsing the suds out while watching her stare. When her eyes start to dip, I say her name in warning, "Belle."

She opens her mouth and closes it so many times, I think she's close to hyperventilating.

"Turn around, Bellamy."

Her pretty face colors as she gasps again, unfreezes, and finally whirls around. "You shouldn't be washing in the waterfall! You've ruined this place for me!"

I toss the two bottles onto shore and start wading out of the water. "We both know that's a lie, babe. Bet you'll be dreaming about it tonight."

Huffing, she starts marching away through the woods.

"Don't leave!" I hop out, forgoing drying off, and yank on my track pants while trying to shove my boots on. "Wait!" Giving up on the boots, I scoop up the sweatshirt and wrestle it on as I take off through the woods. I break past the trees and spot the white truck in the parking lot, its owner yanking the door open.

Ignoring the rocks and junk jabbing into the soles of my feet, I sprint over as she slams the door. Luckily, the window is rolled down so I reach inside and yank the keys out of the ignition.

"Hey!" Bellamy tries to snatch the keys out of my hand but I dodge her and drop them into my pocket.

"Please don't leave." I take a second to finish pulling the shirt down where it's hung up around my chest. "Stay and let's talk." I watch the fight in her deflate as she slumps against the seat. "We can go sit in the glider behind the garage. Just chill together. Just... please stay."

After giving her a minute, I open the door and offer her my hand. Of course, she refuses it, but climbs down and walks past me in the direction of my offer. Things with Bellamy are never how I want them to happen, but, like this instance, I'll take whatever she'll allow. I follow behind her, shoving a hand through my damp hair to get it out of my face, right confused and a little peeved with myself for doing what I swore I'd never do—let a woman rule any part of my life. As I plop down beside Bellamy, I realize that she's gone and done it anyway.

I settle in beside her while trying not to shiver. My flipping toes are like icicles and I'm pretty sure they are all gonna turn black and fall off. The smart thing to do would be to go get a pair of shoes from inside, but I ain't chancing her taking off, so I reach down and yank the bottom of my pant legs over them. This causes my waistband to lower almost too far, reminding me of something else I skipped besides shoes. I'm the cool aloof dude who is normally sure of himself, but at the moment I find myself wrestling with my less-than-enough clothing like a dork. All the while, Bellamy just sits staring off into the distance like I'm not jostling the both of us.

I give up on getting warm and grow still. When she remains quiet, I take her hand in mine and lace our fingers.

"Your skin is like ice," Bellamy whispers while placing her other hand on top of mine to rub some warmth into it. "How can you stand it?"

"There's a fine line between pleasure and pain." I wink at her and she tries to take her hand back, but I hold firm and refuse to let go.

"You're insufferable."

"And you're beautiful." I know I'm egging her on, but it's the only way I've found to pull her out of lockdown mode.

"Bathing in the waterfall is inappropriate," Bellamy fires back, but her voice is flat, so I set in to rile her up.

"No more inappropriate than you gawking at me." I wink again.

"I don't think that's a good idea."

I tsk. "Me either. Watching poor unsuspecting men wash really ain't very ladylike, ma'am."

Her retort this time is a huffy groan, but she barely contains that small smile playing along her pouty lips. That little expression is a victory, so I set the slider into motion and bask in the sunshine and Bellamy allowing me to hold her hand. I glance around, confident enough that no one can see us back here, and sit a little closer to her.

"Where've you been, babe?" I wait for an answer, and when she fails to deliver one, I let go of her hand and drape my arm over her shoulder until she's tucked close to my side. Man, she's a whole lot of warmth to my frozen. "Talk to me."

Bellamy rests her head on my chest and starts fiddling with the strings of my sweatshirt. "I read the letters."

"Ah, Belle. You could have brought them here and we'd have done it together." Without much thought, I kiss the top of her head and hold her a little tighter. She obviously brushed her hair before coming over. It's smooth and silky and danged if I can't keep my fingers from combing through it. "I've told you how many times now?"

"I... I needed to do it on my own."

"No, you didn't. This thing works both ways. You've been there for me ever since you got stuck with me. I'm gonna be there for you too. You stepped into the circle, remember?"

Bellamy takes a deep breath and exhales, and I can feel the heat of it seep through the material of my sweatshirt. "I went to the prison Tuesday."

I almost blurt out that she didn't have to do that on her own either, but stop myself because the stupid thing on my ankle reminds me of my limitations. "How'd it go?" I ask, already knowing the answer. It was bad enough she shut down and hid for several days.

"Waverly planned to kill himself that night..."

"By running into Beau?"

She shakes her head before burying her face in the crook of my neck. Between her touch and my anger over Waverly, the chill from my skin has vanished. "No. He had a gun, but couldn't do it sober. That's why he says he got drunk. He was going to drive somewhere and... Well, he killed Beau and walked away without so much as a scratch."

"How morbidly ironic is that!" I take my own deep inhale, trying to tamp down my temper.

Bellamy doesn't answer, just holds me tighter. There may be limitations to what I can do, but holding her isn't one of them, so I pick her up and settle her across my lap without any protest. I keep the glider in a slow motion, waiting for her to fall apart, but she never does. That's probably what's been going down since Tuesday.

"Have you forgiven your parents?"

Her question catches me off guard and picks at a scab that refuses to go away. I hate how she always goes in a direction I want no part in. "They ain't asked," I answer, hoping to shut this down.

"Is that all that's holding you back from forgiving them?"

I reach back and pull the hood over my head to ward off some of the chill. "I think I'm a pretty understanding kinda guy, willing to give something if asked, but neither one has ever admitted they did anything wrong. Mostly, that makes me think them checking out on me is what I deserved."

"You know that's not true, right?"

My shoulder jerks up. Defensive and over the subject, I try to direct it back to her. "Where are you going with this?"

"I need to forgive Carl Waverly."

"Need?"

"Yes. He's asked for it in all twenty-six letters and on Tuesday. Apparently, I'm not the kinda girl to give what's been asked of me."

"Don't go selling yourself short like that."

Just as I'm about to place a kiss on her forehead, Bellamy lifts her face and the kiss lands on her upper lip. Not wanting to freak her out, I lean away but she follows me. It's all the permission I need, but I don't accept it. For the first time in my life, I put a woman's needs before my own desires. Bellamy doesn't need a kiss from me, she needs my comfort, but she clearly takes it as rejection and tries to withdraw.

I hold her a little tighter and attempt to explain. "Baby, I want to kiss you, but only when you're ready to kiss me for me." I trace the blush on her cheek. "I'm selfish. I ain't down with sharing this kiss with ghosts. When you're ready, we'll only share it between you and me." I place the kiss I intended a moment ago on her forehead and let my lips linger there until she relaxes and seems to come to terms with what I just said. My only worry there is that she'll never want to kiss me now.

"I still love my husband and always will." Her voice is quiet but firm.

"I know that, Bellamy. I'm not telling you to give that up." I loosen my arms, giving her an out. She quickly takes it, leaving me here with my bruised ego. I close my eyes and slump against the swing, not wanting to see her take off, and only know she's gone when the sound of the truck fades.

It might make me the scumbag many say I am, but the truth is, I'm jealous of a dead man. Resentful that he still has this amazing woman's loyalty even from the grave. I've never had that and up until Bellamy slapped my face for the first time, I've never wanted anything but physical gratification from a woman. She makes me want more.

Knowing it ain't happening, I stand up and retrace the path to the waterfall to gather my mess. It isn't until I'm shoving my feet into my boots that I notice No-tail napping on the pile of dirty clothes. At least she brought my cat back so I'm not completely alone. I scoop him up and make my way to the garage. After refilling his food bowl and water, I stretch out on the couch and stare at the ceiling, scanning the Christmas decorations I strung up there without really seeing any of it. All I see is Bellamy. She's there in almost every memory I've gathered in the last several months, both good and bad. The only constant I've had is her being there, something not even my mother and father ever offered me. Shoot, I know she's right. I need to forgive them even if they don't want my forgiveness. It needs to be done so I can finish getting my act together. It's due time. But how?

In the midst of stewing on all that, I somehow manage to doze off, but a loud motorcycle pulling up rouses me out of it. Sitting up and rubbing the sleep from my eyes, I expect Drew to come in with supper just as he's done every late Sunday night since I've been here, but it's not him who cracks open the side door and steps inside.

"Pop?"

"Son." He shoves his hands inside the pockets of his carpenter jeans. The same Dickie brand he's worn for as far back as I can remember, along with the same Harley leather jacket. My love of motorcycles came from him. Guess the taste of alcohol was all from him too.

"What are you doing here?"

"Good to see you, too."

I narrow my eyes at him, not even attempting to hide the irritation he's provoked. "It's the first time you've shown up here, so just cut the crap."

"I had a young lady come to the house tonight. Quite a looker…" He smirks and looks like he has something on me. I hate that I look so much like him, and it makes me wonder if I appear as smarmy as him when I give that look.

Standing up, I file that thought away for later and vow to ditch the smirking. "What'd she say to you?"

"She had a good bit to say, actually. Made me realize I was wrong on a few things." Pop takes a hand out and gestures to the couch. "I think we need to have a long overdue conversation."

I tick my chin once, inviting him over as I move to a chair to keep some space between us. It's the first time we've been in the same space since my hospital visit, when he stayed all of five minutes to make sure I was still breathing. I watch him sit while trying to wrap my mind around Bellamy tracking him down. That woman is a pain in the butt, going to bat for me but refusing when I want to do the same for her. "You were nice to her, right?"

Pop combs a hand through his graying blond hair. "Of course, I was. Son, I don't know when I became the bad guy here, but—"

I let out a derisive snort. "Really? You're really gonna go there? You checked out of life and into a bottle before I even had teen tacked to my age." I tilt my head and squint at him. "Then, wasn't it before graduation you moved out?"

Pop is a beast of a man, taller and broader than me, but right now he looks insubstantial. "I know I didn't handle things well. I thought you were better off without me. And you were." He has enough nerve to motion to the bike in the corner of my jailcell. "You moved out to California and built yourself an empire. You never needed me."

"Yeah, what kid needs their parents." I snort again and roll my eyes. "To hell with parents, right?"

"Lee…"

I hold a palm up and take a deep breath, knowing cussing him with every word in the book won't give me a childhood redo. After a few more breaths, I whisper through the tightness in my throat, "You and Ma forced me to learn how not to need you, but I sure did *want* you."

Even though the words were whispered, they hang heavy in the air and seem to weigh us both down. We grow quiet for a while, staring at the cement floor. I dig the phone out of my pocket and fire off a text to Bellamy. *I'm so ticked at you for this.* Not wanting to deal with her reasoning behind it, I power the phone down and toss it onto the coffee table.

"Look, what's done is done. Can't change it, so you can head on out."

Pop looks up and there are actual tears swimming in his blue eyes. "Can you forgive me, son?"

"Is that what Bellamy told you to say?"

"No. She asked me if I had ever asked you to forgive me, and it made me realize I hadn't. But I thought you were over it."

"Just thought I was over it?" I repeat slowly and then flatten my lips together.

"Like I said, you're larger than life. Living a dream. You seemed to be doing just fine to me."

"You've seen me in the news. My mugshot. Caught a glimpse of me in the hospital bed." I jack the leg of my pants up and rest my foot on the coffee table. "This ankle monitor and all that... Does it look like I'm doing just fine?"

Pop only gives the black contraption on my leg a fleeting glance before going back to staring at the floor.

"What, Pop?" I lift my foot and bang it as hard as I can against the table, sending a cup of pens spilling to the floor. "You don't care to see what's right in front of you? Guess you never have, have you?"

"I've failed you, so yeah, it's hard to face that." He leans forward and scrubs his hands down his face.

"And that right there makes you a coward, leaving your kid to face it all on his own, just because it's *hard*."

He drops his hands and cuts me a look. "You're not a kid anymore."

"Yeah, you and Ma buried my childhood right along with Tommy, making me grow up hard and fast. I should have just climbed inside that casket with him."

Pop's head shakes back and forth. "Please don't bring your brother into this."

"How can I not?" I stab a finger at the ankle monitor before setting my foot on the floor. "It all revolves around losing him. Let's be clear on something here." I shove out of the chair, tipping it over, and smack my chest. "I lost him too!"

"Lee..." Pop huffs, but I ignore him.

"You wanted this conversation, old man, so now you're going to sit there and listen. My pastor helped me understand that every stupid mistake I've made is a product of holding in all the hurt from losing Tommy and from y'all walking away from me. I hold it in, letting it fester until it spills out a whole bunch of ugly all over the place."

I set in to a tight pace around the garage, focusing on what I discussed with Chase this week when we had another talk, so I won't start destroying anything in the room. I turn back to my father. "You never looked past your own grief long enough to see how losing Tommy affected me. Man, it tore some big holes in me." Something else Chase pointed out this week is how I fill those holes with unhealthiness that lands me in jail and on the news. The guy makes a lot of sense.

"I don't know how to make this right, Lee." Pops rises from the couch and walks over to me. "But I want to. Really, son, I'm sorry." His long arms come at me before I can retreat and wrap me in a bear hug. And that's all it takes for me to start crying like I should have well over a decade ago.

Chapter Fourteen

Bellamy

Sleep was an elusive thing last night. Nothing new there since that's become my norm for the last few years, but the reason behind it was different this time. After five unanswered text messages and at least that many ignored phone calls, the message that I overstepped became quite clear. I don't even know what came over me. One minute I was trying to come to terms with forgiving Waverly, and then the next I shut my own issues off and focused on fixing Lee's with his father.

If it was solely up to me I'd already be at the garage on my knees, begging Lee to forgive *me*. Sadly, obligation to the Ladies of Faith has me sitting in this small diner for breakfast at their monthly meeting. It's a small group of elderly widows who have made it their duty to mother me, the youngest member of this widow tribe.

I'm pushing a dollop of scrambled eggs from one side of the plate to the other when Lee's name catches my attention. "What was that, Ms. Mary?"

"I said Lee is donating quilts." She smiles from across the table before taking a sip of coffee.

"For what?"

Ms. Doris clucks her tongue. "Pay attention, dear."

"Honey, you'd know if you didn't skip service last Wednesday night." Ms. Jane gives me a subtle scold over the top of her glasses. "I asked prayer for the nursing home residents who don't have loved ones checking on them. Then we talked about starting a ministry where groups from the church take turns visiting once a month and bringing them a gift of some sort."

"Yes, and that sweet boy came up to us after church and said to give him a list of gift ideas and he'd take care of it. Yesterday, he told me his assistant found enough quilts for the first visit and that next month for Christmas he'd find out a specific gift each resident may need or want." Ms. Mary beams and it's all I can do not to giggle at the notion of her calling that giant rugged man a *sweet boy*— even if what he's doing is beyond sweet.

My stomach suddenly churns, thinking I may have to face the wrath of that sweet boy in a little bit. By the time we finish up at the diner and I take Ms. Mary home, it's close to ten and I'm close to coming unglued.

I quickly park in my usual spot beside the church and make a beeline to the garage. Before I get the door open, Chase calls out my name. I turn and see him striding over.

"He's not there," Chase says before reaching me.

My heart drops. "What? Did he take off? Oh, no! He's in jail, isn't he?" I move away from the garage and meet Chase halfway.

Chase's hands shoo my questions away. "No. Nothing like that."

I motion toward the garage. "Then how is he not here?"

"He's taking a timeout in the woods."

"A timeout?"

"Yes. Sometimes it does a man good to just have some time to himself to think about things, so I encouraged him to do so." Chase leads us to the church and opens the door for me.

"So he's just sitting out there for a while?"

"Drew brought him plenty of camping supplies. I told him to take as many days as he needed."

We stop outside my office as panic sets in about what I may have caused by contacting Thomas Sutton. "Why would Lee need a few days? Is he okay? Did something happen?"

"Calm down, Bellamy." Chase pats my shoulder. "I had a counseling session with Lee and his father this morning. It was tougher on Lee than he anticipated, so that's why he needs this timeout."

"What happened?"

Chase takes a step down the hall. "You know I can't share that with you. Please promise you'll respect his wishes for some space."

With no other choice, I nod and turn to enter my office, but come to a halt. "What about No-tail?"

Chase smiles. "The cat followed him."

"Okay." I watch him disappear into his office down the hall from mine, trying to find comfort in Lee having at least the cat for company. If space is what Lee needs, then that's what I'll give him. I can be patient...

****

A few days later, I'm plumb out of patience as Wednesday night service concludes with no sign of Lee to be found. His timeout has set into motion my own, giving me too much time to second-guess my actions on Sunday night. Drew even warned me when I asked him to help me find Thomas Sutton. Drew is a lanky, tattooed guy who looks nothing like my sun-worn, slightly chubby Meemaw Ama, but he sure sounded like her when he warned me not to poke the bear.

Meemaw moved in with my parents not too long after they were married, which Momma always said was a blessing since Daddy's career as a soldier took him away on deployment quite often. Momma grew up in a small Cherokee community, so moving away was an easier transition once Meemaw was on board with moving with her.

Meemaw is woven into most of the childhood memories I made before she passed away my junior year of high school. She loved to share Native American philosophy with me. While some ideas were too complicated for my adolescent brain to comprehend, I absorbed some and can still hear her willowy voice whispering them in my head.

Healing doesn't mean the damage never existed. It means the damage no longer controls you.

She shared that one with me after my pet rabbit Doodle died.

Certain things catch your eye, but pursue only those that capture your heart.

Meemaw told me that one after my first crush crushed my heart. At only age fourteen, I didn't understand the meaning, but it became absolutely clear after I met Beau McCoy my freshman year at Lee University.

Honestly, I'm only beginning to understand her words on healing. And even though I finally understood pursuing those that capture my heart with Beau, I never thought my lifetime would find me pursuing another.

Meemaw used to love telling me not to poke a bear—mostly when I was trying my mother's patience or when Daddy was napping. I asked her once whether that was one of those philosophies. She said no, it was just good common sense. So when Drew crossed his arms with his brow furrowed and said, "I wouldn't poke that bear if I were you," I couldn't help but think of her. And like I used to do to her when she said it, I ignored Drew just the same.

As I head into the dark woods, I know I'm about to go poke the bear some more, but my patience has run out to the point where I'm willing to face the beast head on. Although I'm trying to be careful to avoid twigs and pinecones, it sounds like Sasquatch is bounding through this small forest. The bear has to know he has company on the way, but as I reach the giant tent near the waterfall, the noise doesn't draw him out of hibernation. The only sign of life is a wisp of smoke rising from the fading camp fire.

Not sure what to do, I grab a small log from the pile beside the newly constructed firepit and toss it on the dwindling fire before sitting beside it. A few moments pass with me regarding the growing flames before a heavy sigh comes from inside the tent. A few more pass and I'm beginning to wonder if he has no plans on coming out when the zipper whirls down.

From my periphery, I catch Lee unfolding himself from the tent but keep my eyes pinned to the fire. He stands off to the other side of the firepit and lets out another long sigh.

"This thing between us ain't working for me," Lee rasps, his voice sounding like it's not been used in quite a while.

Not sure if it's the heat of the fire or embarrassment his words evoked, but sweat collects along my upper lip. Using the back of my hand to dab at it, I finally chance looking at Lee. His broad shoulders always look solid enough to carry the world, yet this evening they are drooped in defeat. The scruff on his face has formed into a thick beard, hiding a good bit of his features, but there's no hiding the dark circles underneath his puffy eyes.

I want to skirt around the fire and wrap my arms around him, but instead stay put and wait for him to elaborate. Here I was ready to pursue him, and he is shooting me down before I can even get a good start.

Lee sends the hood of his coat over his head and sits on the ground across from me. He drapes his arms over his drawn knees and lifts his head just enough to connect our stares. His shadowed appearance would be menacing if he didn't look so sad.

Swallowing past the lump in my throat, I ask, "Things didn't go well with your dad?"

He snuffs a soundless laugh, looking none too humored. "What? Were you expecting we'd just hug it out when you sent him the other night?"

I shake my head. "Of course not. He owed you an apology. I only wanted to help you."

Lee slowly inclines his head until it feels like he's leering down at me even from across the fire. "Like I said, this ain't working. You wiggled your way into my circle and I wanted in yours, but you keep me out."

The wind bristles through the trees, sending the smoke in my direction. Seems like a good enough reason as any to get up and leave. At first, I take a few steps toward that notion, but turn back and stalk over to Lee. "I'm working on me, okay? I've been doing that by using you!"

Lee stands and tilts his head, regarding me with confusion pinching his handsome face. "Using me?"

"Yes..." I look anywhere but at him and try to get my words out in a way that will make sense to the both of us. "You're no better than Waverly. You got yourself intoxicated, and with no regard for other's lives, you drove—"

"So you can't forgive me either."

"No! That's the problem. After all this time with you, I see where your mistake came from. Not saying that makes it right, Lee, but you deserve another chance. A chance where the ghosts of not forgiving your parents won't haunt you. I empathize with you. I have compassion for you." I clutch my chest. "I even love you, but I've struggled with reconciling that with how completely opposite I feel about Carl Waverly. I have to forgive him. I thought if you were strong enough to do it, then maybe I could too."

Lee pushes the hood off his head and combs a hand through his tousled hair. "You just said a whole lot of stuff right then."

"Yeah." I sniff. "I know."

"But I only heard you say you love me." The perpetual pout of his lips softens.

"I'm sorry."

His eyes close as he pushes out a sharp breath. "Please do not apologize for that."

I toss my hands up when he reopens his eyes. "Then what do you want me to do?"

"I want you to say it again."

I could almost swear I hear Meemaw whispering through the breeze. *Pursue those that capture your heart.* I step close and smooth the palm of my hand along the side of his bearded cheek while focusing on his big blue eyes. "I love you."

Lee rocks back on his heels as if those three words just delivered quite an impact. When his arms dart out and wrap around me until I'm firmly cocooned in his warmth, I feel how impactful it was on him. His body trembles, heart pounding against my other palm, breaths racing in and out. I wait for him to offer those three words back to me, but he says nothing. Just holds me and kisses the top of my head like I'm the most precious thing.

He eventually whispers near my ear, "Why me?"

"I have no idea, but I do." I lift my head from his chest and give in to the need to run my fingers through his hair, finding it much softer than I had anticipated for such a hard man.

This time, when I lift my face to his, Lee doesn't lean away. He cups my neck, directing my head to tilt. Those curious blue eyes slowly scan my face, as if savoring the moment. Leaves rustle and the waterfall splashes behind me, but the sounds barely register as we simply hold each other. I'm content with it pausing here when suddenly, his lips crash against mine in a force I've never encountered before now. His moan connects with my gasp, sending a vibration zinging through my body that starts at my lips and travels all the way to my toes.

Everything about this kiss is new to me, from the intensity to the thoroughness, yet there's a familiarity to it. Perhaps sparring with Lee during the last few months is the reason, or maybe it's just the man himself. He oozes charisma and sensuality, and I'm probably being silly to even think it has anything to do with me.

Lee grows still and moves just enough to disconnect our lips by only a breath. "Belle, please tell me you felt that."

"Felt what?" I whisper, hoping to hide how much of an emotional wreck I am.

"I don't know how to say it, but I've never felt what I feel with you."

I want to tell him he only needs three words, but I won't force him into saying it, so I eliminate the space between our lips and kiss him again. As he takes over the kiss, I get this invigorating sense of being on the precipice of what can be anything and everything. Whether it be a small step or an incredible leap, I'm ready to take it on.

The kiss continues until the need to breathe demands a pause, so we break the connection and have a seat on the ground. With my back to Lee's chest, he circles his arms around me and we cuddle by the fire until it starts to die down. I help him gather some stuff and finish putting the campfire out as he tells me about working on reconciling with his father. They plan to meet with Chase once a week for a while.

"What about your mom?"

"That's what I've been out here trying to make peace with. I need to forgive her even if she never asks for it." He shakes a finger at me. "Don't even think about tracking her down like you did with Pop."

"Are you still made at me about that?"

Lee shrugs and gives me a sidelong glance. "Kiss me and I'll forgive you."

I lean up and deliver the kiss, planning on making it short and sweet. The next thing I know everything we were carrying is now scattered at our feet. Breathless, we untangle our arms and take a minute to collect ourselves.

"Best apology I've ever received," Lee mutters to himself while picking up the sleeping bag.

Dizzy and blushing, I gather everything I dropped and start down the path on wobbly legs.

"I actually want to thank you for giving me and my old man the kicks in the butts we needed to work this mess out between us."

"You think the counseling sessions with Chase will help?"

"I've already been spending some time in his office, one on one, and it's helped me, so I hope so. It's been a long time coming, but I'm ready to get my act together."

"I wonder if there's a way Waverly and I could have some counseling sessions together. Not with Chase, but maybe another pastor," I comment as we begin trekking out of the woods with No-tail following.

"I think that's a good idea." Lee stops and waits for me to look up at him. "But don't think for a minute I agree with what he did. You don't owe him anything, but you do owe it to yourself."

People always say I owe this or that to Beau—*you owe it to Beau to carry on without him, you owe it to Beau to keep up this event or that charity, you owe it to Beau not to give up*—but never has anyone told me I simply owe it to myself until now.

Beau...

It suddenly strikes me that this is the first time I thought about Beau in the last hour, and that realization delivers a mixed bag of emotions. I'm proud of myself for making progress, but right behind that my insides pinch with guilt. And then the guilt is shoved to the side by an overpowering affection as Lee places an arm around my shoulder, presses his lips to my forehead, and begins walking again.

We drop off his belongings inside the garage, and Lee walks me to the truck. Before I climb in, he cups my face and tilts it until I'm staring up at him. "The kiss... you okay?"

"I think, for the first time in a very long time, I'm okay."

Lee delivers one of his genuine smiles as he leans in and gives me the most delicate kiss I've ever received. Feather soft, yet boy, does it pack a punch.

"I think, for the first time *ever,* I'm okay," he whispers against my lips before pressing them to mine once more. "Good night."

I load up, feeling like a shy schoolgirl on the brink of a fit of giggles. "Good night."

And it truly is a good night. I sleep soundly for the first time in over two years, proving that I really am okay. Meemaw's words hold true as they always have. *Healing doesn't mean the damage never existed. It means the damage no longer controls you.*

Chapter Fifteen

Lee

The last several Thanksgivings haunt me today like the ghost of Christmas past does with Ebenezer Scrooge from that movie. Like it gets some twisted satisfaction from showing him all the awfulness he took part in while Scrooge looks ready to keel over from embarrassment. Wait, no... Maybe that's just me... I'm repulsed just thinking about the way I've used the holiday for self-pleasure. The same suite was booked each year in Vegas and the plans were always the same—blow obscene amounts of money while guzzling ridiculously overpriced whiskey and notching my belt with as many female conquests as fit my mood.

This Thanksgiving, as I dish out another serving of dressing to a kid from the local shelter home, I think about those past Thanksgivings with a much different perspective. I used to feel prideful over those trips, like it was my way of giving my parents the middle finger for all the missed holidays. This year, all I feel is shame over how I've carried on.

"Whoa, sir. I don't think I can eat that much." The kid's eyes are rounded like saucers, drawing my attention to the fact that I just covered half his plate with dressing.

"Just eat what you can and I'll get you a container for whatever's left, so you can take it with you."

He grins, showing off several crooked teeth that need more regular brushings. "Thank you."

You would have thought I gave him the moon instead of extra food, and giving him just that slice of happiness gives me more pleasure than anything I ever found in Vegas. The fifteen grand I lost in one card game comes to mind as my eyes catch on the duct tape holding his sneaker together as the kid walks away. After watching him sit back down, I scan the fellowship hall and take in each child feasting away. Most are in need of a haircut and a new wardrobe. That money I threw away could have provided each one with those needs.

"That's the last of it." Asher knocks into my arm as he passes by with the empty sweet potato casserole pan.

"Man, you sure know how to cook." His restaurant provided the food today. All we had to do was serve it up and try not to eat too much of it ourselves.

Asher grunts for a response like he normally does if someone compliments him, or attempts to shoot the breeze with him, or any other time a conversation tries including him for that matter.

"Nice talking to you as always," I smart off, earning a sharp side-eye from the mostly mute man before he disappears into the kitchen.

Leaving him alone, I go back to dishing out dressing and mulling over my mess. Once the pan is empty and I've gotten a pretty good estimate of how much money I've wasted in Vegas over the last three years, I let Bellamy know I'll be in the kitchen. I take a minute to shoot the estimated amount to my accountant with instructions to donate that much to the children's home, carefully expressing that it's to be used for clothing and personal care products. Even after he replies he'll take care of it, I feel no better. I know cutting a check won't atone for my sin, but those kids need the money and I have it to give. I'd buy them all a new life if it were possible, but at least Valley Church has these programs set up to help. I'm just thankful I get to be a part of something that matters on this holiday.

I look down at my shirt, where the gray thermal is speckled with orange pumpkins, wondering how I managed to matter to so many.

"Yo, I'm heading out." Drew walks over with an empty pie pan in one hand and a spatula in the other, setting both down on the table once he reaches me.

I scrape a crusty corner of dressing from the pan and prepare to shove it into my mouth. "Why don't you stick around?"

"For what?"

"The service," I garble out and shrug a shoulder.

"Are you suggesting or demanding?"

I chew the mouthful of dressing, recalling all the times he's asked the exact same question over the years. The kid has always wanted clarity on what's required of him and it makes me pause and wonder if I've been too hard on him. In this case, I know it wouldn't sit well with me if someone demanded I attend a service of any sort, so I give him an out and hope he doesn't take it.

"I'm inviting you to stay, but if you don't want to hang out with the most popular guy here, it's your loss." I tip my chin up and smack a hand against the gazillion stickers dotting my shirt.

"You cheated by bribing those kids with giant portions of food."

"I'm nice like that. You would've gotten at least one sticker if you hadn't been so dang stingy with the pie," I mouth off as Bellamy joins us. She's dressed casual in fitted jeans and a dark-green sweater, and it's taking all my willpower today not to steal a kiss.

She catches me staring at her and winks, and that right there makes my stomach tighten. Then she goes and presses her sticker to the arm of Drew's shirt.

"Drew, you can sit with me instead of Mr. Popular. I'd love your company."

Drew cuts his eyes at me, looking too smug for my liking, as he offers Bellamy his arm. He's staying for the service, which is all I wanted, so I'll let him think he's one-upped me for once.

I follow behind them as they head over to the church where most of the group has already migrated. It's a mix of youth group members and the children's home residents along with a good many adults. Bode and Mia are here but have kept their distance as they do at most services I attend. I reckon I don't blame them. If someone made a serious play for Bellamy, I don't think I'd handle it as well as Bode did when I tried toying with his wife. The closer Bellamy and I become, the more I understand why I need to properly voice that apology to both Bode and Mia.

"So, is there anything behind these stickers? The person with the most gets a turkey or something?" Drew asks while holding the sanctuary door open for Bellamy like the gentleman I didn't know he could be.

I step in before he lets go of the handle, but the punk is quick to take his spot back beside Bellamy.

"The sticker is a tradition we started several years ago. During the service, each person stands up. For each sticker they received, they have to share something they are thankful for."

Drew snorts a laugh and glances over his shoulder at my shirt. Guess the joke is on me. I sit on the row behind them and take in all the pumpkins stuck to me, wondering if I can come up with enough things I'm thankful for to cover all of them.

Chase starts off by asking those who have received one sticker to stand up and share. About a half dozen people stand up and say what they are thankful for, mostly their health or family. I give Drew's shoulder a shove when he doesn't stand, sending him slowly to his feet.

"How about you, Drew? What are you thankful for?" Chase asks.

149

Drew keeps his back to me while answering, "I'm thankful Lee took me in when most of the world shut me out." He sits faster than I've ever seen him move and slumps as if he's trying to hide from what he just shared.

Stunned by his words, it makes me want to lean up and hug him for the first time ever. Instead, I clamp him on the shoulder and give it a squeeze before letting go.

Stuck on what Drew just said, I barely hear what anyone else says until Chase calls my name. I look up and see him motioning for me to stand.

"I believe you have the most stickers. How about getting started on what all you're thankful for." Chase nods in encouragement.

Clearing my throat, I pluck the first sticker off and hold it up. "I'm thankful y'all like me so much."

Everyone laughs at this, so I pluck another one off to keep it rolling. With a glance over my shoulder, I spot Asher and Neena on their usual pew in the very back. She grins and he frowns at me. "I'm thankful Asher Reid can cook like a boss." This earns a round of applause and the big guy's face turns red.

I continue, "I'm thankful for probably being the first person in history to be sentenced to house arrest at a church."

I look up with a smirk, expecting another round of laughter but only meet up with dead silence. *Tough crowd.* I glance at Chase and he points to my chest, wanting me to continue.

After peeling another one off, I say a little quieter, "I'm thankful Chase McCoy has a heart and let it and Neena Reid convince him to give me this opportunity." Another sticker is removed. "I'm thankful I didn't physically hurt anyone but myself when I drove drunk." Swallowing hard, I pluck another one off. "I'm thankful Bellamy McCoy has helped me to understand how detrimental my actions could have been on an innocent family. How my actions do impact those around me, good or bad."

I take another sticker off and look over at the Calder family, waiting until Bode looks at me. "I'm thankful to be welcomed even though I don't deserve it. And I'm thankful to those who have prayed for me when they have had every right not to."

There are at least five more stickers but I conclude with saying, "I'm thankful to spend this Thanksgiving here with y'all. Best one I've had in a long time." My body feels too heavy to keep holding it up so I ease back onto the pew and stare down at my boots.

"Thank you for sharing with us, Lee. I'm thankful for God blessing me with the opportunity to get to know the remarkable man you really are. I just hope the world has the opportunity to get to know the real you after your time with us concludes."

Someone stands up front and starts leading the group in some praise songs, but I remain seated and work on blinking the burning from my eyes to no avail. When the burning progresses to my nose, fat tears escape. I slap them away and fight against whatever is building up inside my chest. It doesn't work, so I rest my arms on the pew in front of me and place my forehead on top.

Okay, God, you want it then you can have it. I can't carry this any longer.

And I don't know what was in those words I just prayed but it's like my chest just opens up and the weight I've been carrying around releases.

Please forgive me. Please...

I pray, I beg, I cry, and then repeat it all over again when all of a sudden I'm not in the pew alone any longer. Surrounded by people murmuring prayers on my behalf, God shows me I'm not alone in this.

Hands are touching my back from different directions as prayers and whispers of praise ring out from the crowd, but my eyes fly open when someone slips their hand in mine. I know it's Bellamy practically by her touch alone, yet I can hardly believe she's openly holding my hand. Her pretty pink lips are moving with her own silent prayer.

I've lost a lot due to my stupidity and have no idea why God is granting me so much in the place of it. I think it's time I forgive myself and start owning it.

Chapter Sixteen

Bellamy

Routine is something I've grown leery of over the years. It can trick you into thinking everything is fine just the way it's rolling along, until the unexpected pops up and shatters your false sense of security. I know there is a risk to settling into the temporary routine Lee has here and having him near all the time.

I also should know to be prepared for the unexpected with this man by now, but for some reason I keep letting him trip me up. I reach to open the side door of the garage to see if he wants to join me for my early morning run as he has been doing most mornings for a while now, but Lee opens it and steps outside before I can knock. Judging by the fact that he's barefooted and in a rumpled undershirt and pajama pants, it looks like I'm having a solo run this morning.

"Are you sick?"

"No," he whispers and rubs the sleep from his eyes.

"Why are you whispering?" I crane my neck to peep over his shoulder but he moves to block me. "Is someone in there? You know the rules." I push past him and yank the door open but come to a halt.

Lee's tent is set up in the middle of the garage. I bend slightly to look inside and see two small lumps bundled in their sleeping bags on top of air mattresses.

Lee pulls me outside by the back of my jacket, but not before I spot Drew sprawled on the couch snoring. After Lee closes the door I ask, "What's all over Drew's face?"

"Nothing that won't wash off," Lee whispers with a gravelly voice, sounding like he should go back in there and join his little sleepover for more rest himself. "The boys got wild after he passed out and took markers to his face." Lee tsks. "Little devils."

"You say that with a little too much pride." I smirk. "What are they doing here anyway?"

"Nichole needed a night to herself. I offered for them to stay here. Don't worry. Chase approved it." Lee reaches out and pulls me into his arms. Even though I'm bundled in more layers, he's so warm. "Chase also approved for me to go on a date tonight."

I stiffen in his arms. "A date? But you're not allowed to leave... and... and you can't have a woman over."

He squeezes me closer in his strong arms. "Babe, did you forget you're a woman?"

"No."

"Good. Then meet me in the parking lot tonight at seven." Lee nuzzles my neck, sending sparks to tickle my skin.

"What about today?"

"I'm having a boys day. The Men's Group are meeting today because Mr. James is having hernia surgery tomorrow. I want the boys and Drew to properly meet them."

Lee wanting that with the guys makes me happier than him asking me out on a date. "Lee Sutton, you just keep surprising me." I reach up on my tiptoes and kiss him.

After returning it with much more attentiveness, he eases back. "That's good right?"

"Yes." I steal another kiss and start walking backwards.

"Tonight at seven," he states and points a finger at me.

"You didn't ask," I tease, taking a few more steps away.

"Nope. Don't plan on it either." Lee winks before slipping inside the garage.

Ready to get the day underway so the night gets here faster, I turn around and jog over to the track.

After spending way too long deciding what to wear on my first date in what seems like forever, I go with a pair of dark jeans, a thick knit sweater in a charcoal color and a pair of tall black boots.

With a sudden case of the jitters, I hop in the truck and make the quick drive to the church. I turn into the parking lot, and once I see the motorcycle with its handsome owner straddling it, my nerves vanish. He's wearing a worn leather jacket, a beanie pulled over his blond hair, jeans and his ever-present boots. The scene could be viewed as intimidating if I'd not gotten to know the man behind the tattoos and leather.

I waste no time exiting the truck and moving over to where the motorcycle is idling. It's my favorite one of all the bikes that have rotated through the garage in the last several months. The very one that was delivered in ruins but gradually was made whole again. It fits Lee perfectly, both literally and figuratively.

"Climb on, Belle, so I can take you for a ride."

If Lee wants to spend the evening doing laps around the field or parking lot then that's fine by me, but after I'm settled on the bike behind him, I'm surprised when he takes off toward our little trail through the woods. He takes the small trek slowly and I notice a warm glow shining through the trees even before we make it to the waterfall.

"How on earth did you pull this off?" I ask after he turns the motorcycle off. I crane my neck to gaze up at the thousands of lights twinkling from where they are strung along the high tree branches.

"You hear that humming?" Lee tilts his head as if listening for it, too. I nod when I catch the subtle sound penetrating past the rushing waterfall. "It's a generator."

"You did all this by yourself?"

Lee gathers my hand in his, helps me off the bike, and then leads me over to a wooden pergola where even more lights show off the table set underneath. "I put the Men's Group to work today. They helped assemble the pergola in no time while Drew and I handled stringing up the lights. And Gavin and Gatlin set the table."

I groan. "So they know about our date?"

Lee uses his grip on my hand to pull me into his side. "You have a problem with them knowing?"

"I guess not. It's just... I like my privacy and this is new to me."

He peers down at me for a few beats before moving us to the table. "I don't want to hide what we have, but I'll respect whatever you want."

"What do we have?" I sit in the chair he pulls out for me and love it when he leans down to place a kiss on the side of my neck before scooting the chair in.

"It feels like to me we have anything we want it to be." Lee reaches inside a thermal tote and comes back with two thermoses. He hands me one and places the other on his side of the table. He reaches in again and this time he pulls out two to-go containers.

I pop open my container and the fluffy pancakes, bacon, and hash browns inside are definitely not what I expect. A sniff from the thermos indicates it's coffee. "Breakfast for supper?"

Lee sets a bottle of maple syrup beside my plate. "It's the only thing I know how to cook."

I glance up in surprise. "You cooked this for me, Lee?"

"Sure did, babe. Even added some cinnamon to the pancakes." He gives me a boyish smile I had no idea he could pull off, and then bows his head and says grace.

We eat in silence for a little while as I take in all the details of our first date. The table has a crisp white tablecloth dressing it. In the center is a silver lantern and a small arrangement of orange and dark-pink roses. Breakfast may be the only thing he knows how to cook, but it's like anything else Lee decides to take on—done with careful precision. I take another bite, marveling in the perfection of the spicy sweet pancakes.

"Lee?" I ask before taking a sip of coffee with a subtle hint of spice to it. The man sure does like that for some reason.

"Yeah, babe?" he asks, sounding distracted.

"What do you want from what we have?" I motion between us with my fork.

He reaches over to adjust the setting on the standup propane heater set up beside the table and then turns his attention to me. "You have a pretty good idea of the man I am by this point. I don't do anything halfway. I'm all in when it comes to something that's important to me." He slowly grazes the tips of his fingers over the top of my hand where it rests beside my plate, sending a shiver up my arm. "I know you feel that. We have some kind of crazy chemistry, but this goes a lot deeper than that."

I'm unable to meet his eyes, so I keep watching his long fingers trace patterns on top of my hand. "So... What do we do with it?"

"You're the first woman I've had more than a physical relationship with. Honestly, it's surprised me how much I enjoy you. You're kind even when it's not deserved. You have a stellar sense of humor, but you're a little stingy with sharing that quality. And I really dig the way you've let me be something important to you. For now, I think we keep exploring it." His hand retreats as a long sigh escapes him. "I'm here for a few more months, but I want you to be willing to give my real world a chance when I move back home."

Unable to take another bite, I set the fork down and can't help but worry he doesn't view this as real enough. "You miss your real world?"

"Just my home, and the freedom to go see Gavin and Gatlin any time I want. I have my work and my crew stops in almost every other day, so all that is still the same. I'm pretty sure you're going to go running in the other direction as soon as the paparazzi and the stuff that comes with the celebrity part of my life gears back up. It can be intense."

I shrug. "I guess we'll figure it out."

"I hope you'll be willing." Lee sounds more worried than me.

Feeling the need to change the subject, I ask, "Did Drew get the marker off his face?"

Lee chuckles. "Mostly. You should have heard Harvey and Clarence tease him about it. They've made him an honorary Men's Group member since he is already sporting a white beard and hair."

I grin, just imagining that group of guys welcoming the slightly awkward Drew in their own special way. "How'd he take it?"

"He held his own just fine. Especially when he started critiquing their dishes."

We talk about the various takes the men had on oatmeal. Then Lee fills me in about the sleepover with his nephews. I enjoy how easy conversation comes with talking to him, but then he pulls another subject change and dives into a concerning matter fast enough to give me whiplash.

"You haven't told me how your visit with Carl went on Saturday."

"Same as the last two visits. It was uncomfortable and neither of us seem to know how we're supposed to act." I close the lid of the plate just to have something to do. "We sat there for the first ten minutes not saying a word. Finally, I just started rambling on and on about Beau's mission trips. I have no idea why I shared something so personal with a stranger, but before I left, Carl thanked me." I shake my head and slowly blink. The visits rattle me and leave me more confused than before. "I'm not sure if it's a good idea to keep going there."

"Don't give up on it yet." Lee stands and places the containers in the thermal bag. He picks the table up and places it just outside the perimeter of the pergola.

I remain in my chair, baffled by what he's doing, but let out a squeal when he picks up my chair with me still in it like I weigh nothing. Not the case, because I'm pretty sturdy. "What are you doing?"

"I just took my hot date out to dinner. Now I'm taking her dancing." Lee brushes a kiss against my lips just as he puts the chair down. We both snicker when we notice our lips are sticky from the syrup. Lee, being Lee, licks the syrup off my lips before doing the same with his. "Dang, babe, that tasted better than my awesome pancakes."

"The pancakes were delicious, but I think I'll have to agree with you on that."

Lee gives me a heated look, then sets his phone beside a wireless speaker. Adele begins singing words about love and the angst of it before he turns around. In two long strides, he's pulling me to my feet.

"I wouldn't have taken you for an Adele fan." I lace my fingers behind his neck, reveling in the heat along the edge of his beanie.

"The woman can sing. No denying it. I figured she was a better choice for slow dancing than the heavy metal I usually listen to." He moves us in a languid circle, slow and sensual. "You look so beautiful tonight, Belle. So, so beautiful."

"Thank you." Blushing, I lower my head against his chest and keep time to the rhythm of his heartbeats.

Adele serenades us through three songs as the tension builds to the point of not needing the fancy heater to keep warm. Lee holds me in a way that makes me feel safe and appreciated, and I try not to compare this with what I had with Beau, but find my thoughts drifting there anyway.

Although they love differently, there's no denying I've been blessed with the gift of falling in love with two exceptional men. Beau was more cautious and boyish with his affection, but it was just as deep as Lee's more intense, primal style.

Lee touches my chin, lifting my face until I meet his eyes. His vibrant blue starbursts glow under the twinkling lights. It's so hypnotic that I'm unable to close my eyes when he leans in and presses his lips to mine. The new sensation of kissing while holding each other's stare is such an exhilarating experience that I'm spellbound.

As the kiss continues, Lee guides us until my back presses against one of the pergola posts. I expect him to take over and send this moment into a more intense speed, but he does the unexpected and slows everything down to such a tender touch. Slower but no less passionate. So many firsts. So much unexpectedness.

Grazing his knuckles along my cheek, Lee eases the kiss to a close. "Bellamy..." My name is barely an audible rasp. "I..." He begins but something seems to catch his attention. He wraps a protective arm around me while looking around the small clearing. I look too but find nothing out of the ordinary. "I better take you back to the church."

His pronunciation of the *I* is different than the first one he rasped out, making me think he was close to telling me he loved me. I don't understand why he's struggling with voicing what he so easily expresses to me with each touch. He says it so freely to his nephews, so that's not an all-around problem.

The ride back proceeds with more speed than earlier, and I'm climbing off the bike quicker than I wish. Once Lee helps me into the truck, I turn in the seat and say, "Thank you for taking me on a date, Lee. I had a wonderful time."

He scans the parking lot and then leans inside the cab to lay one meaningful kiss on me. "I did too. You get your pretty self home and once you're tucked in bed, I want you to think about me." Winking one of those blue eyes, Lee steps away and shuts the door.

I wish I could take him home with me. Since that's not even possible at this point, I go home and do as he says. I relive each moment of our date until I drift off to sleep.

Chapter Seventeen

Lee

"This thing could be used as a hockey puck." Drew drops the stone-shaped biscuit onto the plate, then picks up the next greasy-looking sample. He takes a bite, chews thoughtfully, and then shakes his head while studying it. "Someone was heavy handed with the shortening. Y'all need to watch that with your old tickers."

"You already tried them all. Which one wins?" Clarence asks, running out of patience with their newly appointed taste-tester.

"None of them are really all that good, but..." Drew points to the speckled biscuit. "That one with the bacon. *Hello.*"

The men chuckle while Wade looks smug as he rearranges his bacon biscuits. At least one of them has figured out the winning ingredient.

"Anything with bacon wins every time!" Harvey bellows.

"Looks like y'all would catch on eventually." I finish off a cheese biscuit that I actually like better than the one with bacon and down the rest of my coffee. "Men, it's been real as always, but I need to get to work before the boss lady gets ahold of me for slacking off."

"You're the least slacking off person I know," Jeb comments.

I stand from the table, pat him on the shoulder, and salute the rest of them before heading outside to tackle the Christmas decorations. The chill in the air has turned almost frigid, so I finish zipping my coat, shove the beanie over my ears, then flip the hood of the coat over it.

"What's first?" Drew says from behind me.

I didn't realize he followed me outside. "You can hang out with the guys. I got this."

"If you're going to volunteer some time, I guess it wouldn't hurt me to do the same." Drew unwraps a sucker, pops it in the corner of his mouth, and pulls on a pair of gloves.

"This is part of a court order, remember? You don't have to." I walk the line of decorations I have arranged on the ground in front of the garage.

"Dude, you forget you've schooled me on how to pay attention to details. So don't think I haven't kept up with your service hours. You're past done with them, yet you keep at it every day just the same."

"What's your point?"

"My point is pretty clear. For such a detail man, you miss some pretty big things sometimes." Drew adjusts a floppy knit cap and then picks up Baby Jesus. "I look to you on how to be a man."

I'm not even that much older than him, and know for a fact I've been a poor example. "Drew, I'm the last guy you need to be studying for that."

"You ain't perfect by no means, but you have the drive to want to be. I've been studying you since the day you took me in, but lately I've learned a pretty big lesson from you." He holds Baby Jesus a little higher. "You've shown me there's much more to this life than what I've been living. Thanks for that."

I watch him take off to the front of the church where I've already placed the manger, trying not to get choked up like a sissy. I roll my neck a few times, sniff back the weak moment, and pick up a shepherd who weighs a ton.

"I still cannot believe you bought a new nativity set. There was nothing wrong with the old one." Bellamy hurries over, takes the shepherd's feet, and helps carry him to the front of the church. She's all bundled up, looking warm and inviting.

"The other set was plastic."

"So." She grunts and adjusts her hold, so I tip most of the weight of the statue back to me. I'd tell her I can do it on my own, but that would be a waste of breath. Stubborn woman.

"Don't these look nicer?" We both study the hand-carved wooden statue.

"They're beyond nicer, and I've seen the prices of these wood carvings." She gives me a pointed look, one that Chase doles out too when I spend money. But it's mine to spend however I want. I've blown enough of it on frivolous nonsense, so it feels good to use my earnings for something significant.

"We need to support local artisans." I ease the statue out of her hold and set it just outside the stable.

"I've seen these carvings all my life, but still cannot believe a chainsaw can do this." She leans her pretty face near it and inhales. "I love the scent of them, too."

I give it a good sniff. "Yeah, it's alright, but give me the scent of cinnamon any day over this." I wink and am satisfied when an attractive shade of pink heats her cheeks.

"Hey, hey," Drew drawls out. He looks and sounds more hillbilly than I do even though he was born and raised on the streets of L.A.

"Good morning, Drew," Bellamy replies while dusting her gloved hands together. "Did the men cook you up something good this morning?"

Drew rolls the sucker to the other side of his mouth before answering. "Biscuits."

As they discuss the merits of a good biscuit, I head back to the garage. My phone buzzes, so I pull off a glove and fish it out of my coat pocket. The screen flashes a text from Lance–*Call me ASAP.*

I put the phone back into my pocket and pick up a sheep. Before I make it over to the stable, my phone goes off another time and then starts ringing. I hand Drew the statue, pull the phone out, and switch it to mute without checking the messages. There's more important things to do than listen to my lawyer rattle off excuses as to why I remain on house arrest. Again, I don't even care anymore.

"Just a few more animals and then all we have to do is scatter a couple bales of hay around it." I motion for Drew to lead the way. Once he takes off in the direction of the garage, I pull Bellamy to the other side of the stable and give her a quick peck on the lips. She giggles and squirms out of my hold, but grabs my hand as we walk over to join Drew.

By the time we've spread the hay and have discussed a strategy for hanging the garlands and lights on the church, I'm feeling in the Christmas spirit. I wish my nephews were here to help do this, but school doesn't let out until next week. I decide to have Drew buy a tree and stuff for the garage so they can help me decorate it this weekend. I'll even invite Bellamy and see if she won't mind making some cookies and hot chocolate.

A familiar car pulls up as I'm unraveling a new strand of lights and thinking over my plans.

"Your favorite person is here," Drew comments while selecting a fresh fir wreath from the pile I had delivered earlier.

"Guess it's time for the monthly visit," I grumble as Officer Abrams climbs out of his patrol car. It's routine for him to show up, look at my ankle monitor like it's going to tell a secret, and grunt out a few warnings before disappearing until the next month.

Resigned to get it over with, I set the lights down and meet him by his car.

"Yo, man. You bring me a Christmas present?" I joke but he glares as always.

I notice he's not carrying his little folder today, and before I can question it, he unsnaps the case on his thick belt that holds the handcuffs.

"Never mind. I don't want any gifts," I joke some more, surprised he's finally showing a dash of sense of humor.

When he pulls them out, I catch on and frown. I yank up the leg of my pants and glare at the monitor. "This thing hasn't gone off one time and you know it."

"There are other stipulations that can violate the order."

"What's going on?" Drew walks over with Bellamy following. I give him a shrug because I have no clue.

Office Abrams ignores him and twirls a hand, indicating he wants me to turn around.

"You're not going to tell me what I did wrong?"

"Not here. No. Turn around and place your hands on the hood."

"I'll go willingly, man. No need for all this."

"He hasn't done anything wrong," Bellamy protests, but I know he's not budging.

Out of the corner of my eye, I see Lance's SUV swinging into the parking lot and then a few news vans start lining the other side of the street. "What the..." I straighten but Abrams shoves me back down onto the hood.

"You'll want to hurry this along before this place becomes a zoo."

"Then just let me get in the back and we'll go. You ain't gotta handcuff me." I know it's no use, because he's clearly out to make a point.

Before Abrams has the handcuffs secured around my wrists, all hell breaks loose. In a blink, the parking lot is swarmed by camera crews and paparazzi.

"Is this some kind of ambush?" Drew asks.

Lance runs up to the car. "Just do as he says, Lee, and we'll sort this out at the station. Hurry up, Abrams!"

"Drew, get Bellamy inside!" I yell, knowing they're still standing somewhere close but can't see them with this overzealous cop pushing my head to the side of the hood while he rattles off my Miranda Rights.

When he yanks me upright by the hood of my jacket, I look around, wondering who sold me out. I hope whoever it was got a pretty penny for it at least. He shoves my head with more force than necessary to help me into the back of the cop car. As he slams the door, my gaze lands on Bellamy. She's pale, no small feat for her warm skin tone, and her bottom lip is trembling.

I mouth, "I'm sorry," but she doesn't acknowledge it. Giving her the benefit of the doubt and chalking it up to shock, I mouth, "I love you." For some reason this seems to snap her out of it and sends her to straight-up irate.

Shaking her head, Bellamy snatches her arm out of Drew's grasp and storms inside the church.

Please let me be wrong. Please don't let her be walking away from me when I need her the most. I silently pray all the way to the police station, and keep doing it through being booked, strip-searched, and placed in a dank jailcell.

Hours tick by before they allow Lance back to see me. On a heavy sigh, he sits beside me on the cot but remains quiet.

"Just give it to me straight." I catch his nod in my periphery, but keep staring at the cinderblock wall in front of me.

"Someone got wind of where you've been serving house arrest. Late last night, a string of photos started popping up all over on the Internet... I'm not going to lie, Lee, it doesn't look good for you."

I snap my head around to face him. "I ain't done anything wrong."

"The pictures tell a different story..." He huffs. "You couldn't stay away from a woman, could you?"

I'm about to punch him in his face when he opens a folder and produces a stack of pictures. He shoves them in my hands, and the one on top makes my stomach pitch. I had a feeling that night someone was watching us, and the image of me holding Bellamy against the pergola post while kissing her is proof. I shuffle through the stack—me carrying Bellamy away from the track after she fell, her on the back of my bike, me leaning into the cab of her truck, us walking across the parking lot while holding hands. Someone has captured each and every moment I've spent with her that I thought was private.

I'm stewing over a statement release to explain the photos, but when I come to one in particular, I know my fate is already sealed. It's me washing in the waterfall while Bellamy stands on the bank. The way her hands are perched on her hips could be misconstrued as her about to take off her top.

"Please make sure no one is harassing Bellamy. Assign a bodyguard to her." I hand the folder back, not wanting to see intimate moments that were monumental to me and are now forever tainted by vindictive members of the media.

"You want to explain these pictures?"

"They're none of your business."

"I'm your lawyer."

I cut him a hard look. "Nothing happened that was inappropriate." I point at his scrunching face. "See! It doesn't matter what I say, no one will believe me."

"Can you blame me for being skeptical?" He holds up the waterfall picture.

I snatch it out of his hand, rip it in half, and toss it at him. "It was an innocent mistake. She happened to walk up on me and was actually fussing at me about washing in the waterfall. You can believe me or not. Don't care. Everything is ruined anyway." Slumping against the wall, I scrub my hands down my face.

"You think it was someone from your crew?"

"You're the one who drafted the confidentiality agreements they've all signed. They'd be stupid to pull something like this."

"I'll find out who did it." Lance tucks the folder into his briefcase.

"What's done is done. Just leave it be."

"Look, Lee, don't let this break you. We'll figure out how to fix it."

What Lance doesn't realize is the only part of this I'm concerned about is losing Bellamy. I glance at the clock on the wall outside my cell. It's been over three hours, so I'm pretty sure she's seen the smear campaign by now. There will be no fixing it.

Clearing my throat, I ask, "When do I go before the judge?"

He sighs again. "Pruitt is out of town until the day after tomorrow. I'm sorry, but you'll have to sit tight for a few days."

I pick at a loose stitch near the knee of my faded jumpsuit. "There isn't another judge in the county?"

"You know Judge Pruitt is assigned to this case."

I raise a palm. "Never mind. Just go do me a solid and make sure Bellamy is okay. And make sure no one at the church is being harassed. Threaten lawsuits if they are."

Lance stands and straightens his tie. "Lee, I'm sorry I didn't see this one coming. I truly thought we placed enough crumbs out there to make the media think you were out at your cabin."

"I know, man. No worries." I hitch a shoulder dismissively.

He takes the hint and turns to leave. "I know this will sound weird, considering you're sitting in jail and all, but, Lee, I'm proud of you and impressed by the transformation you've undergone since this summer."

"Aww, honey, stop before you make me cry," I deadpan.

Lance shakes his head and tosses a hand in the air, either in defeat or to say goodbye, probably both, and leaves well enough alone.

I remain frozen in place on the cot, listening to the clock tick each and every second off of the next hour before I hear the door down the hall being unlocked. Drew strolls up and braces both hands on the bars in front of him.

"Let me outta here! I'm innocent!" He whisper-yells with enough theatrics to send my eyes to rolling. "No? Too soon?"

I keep giving him a blank stare until he drops his hands and shoves them into his pockets. "What are you doing here?"

"I'm here for you to tell me what I need to do."

"I don't even know." I stand up, stretch out my back, and lean against the wall near the bars separating us.

"Good. 'Cause I do." Drew takes out a sucker, and after it's positioned in the corner of his mouth, he fills me in. "I booked Nichole and the boys on a flight down to Florida. That way they can visit Mickey and not be dragged into this mess." He glances over his shoulder at the wall clock. "She should be picking them up from school as we speak. I called up your security company and had a team assigned to the church. Bellamy refused to go to Disney, so I had them assign a team to her, too."

"Thanks, man."

"And I know you didn't want anyone knowing about it and you can fire me or punch me or whatever, but I leaked information about the rehabilitation foundation you've been working on with Chase."

I push off the wall. "Why?"

"Because I'm sick of everyone getting their kicks from tearing you down, and I'm even more sick of you letting them."

"That foundation isn't for me to get a star by my name. It's so others can get a second chance at fixing their lives and the mess they've made with innocent people." It came to me while watching Bellamy struggle with wanting to help Carl Waverly. "Besides, what do you really think people are going to pay attention to, a foundation for prisoners or the money shot of me buck-naked in a waterfall?"

"Yeah..." Drew smirks around the sucker in his mouth. "The water must have been *really* cold." Leave it to him to razz me in this of all moments.

I snort. "Whatever, man."

He grows serious. "So, what's going to happen with you?"

"I'm probably going to prison for a while." I rest my forehead against the coolness of one of the bars. "The pictures look like I've been womanizing and gallivanting around instead of serving a house arrest, which violates my parole. The shots of Bellamy and me riding around the running track on my bike have been cropped in a way that makes it look like we're heading down a highway."

"But the ankle monitor can prove you haven't."

"You'd think, but I have a feeling they're going to insinuate I've tampered with it somehow..." I lift my head and then tap it a few times against the bar. "Man, I've screwed up..."

"By falling for a terrific woman. Nah. This other crap is just mix-ups that'll eventually work out."

I straighten and ask, "She alright?"

"Boy is she one ticked off person at the moment. Said to tell you how gutless it was to finally tell her you love her before being carted off to jail." Drew shakes his head. "That was low, man."

I rub my neck and stare at the floor, knowing he's absolutely right. "She know about the pictures yet?"

"I'm not sure. After she gave me that message, she loaded up in her truck and went straight home."

"It's going to be a few days before I'm brought to see the judge. Just keep an eye on her for me, okay?"

"I will." Drew glances down the hallway. "I'll find out if and what I can bring you before I head out. You gotta be starving. Anything in particular you want for supper?"

"I don't need anything and I'm sure they'll eventually get around to giving me something to eat."

Drew's brows pinch. "You ain't getting sick too, are ya?"

"No. Just sick of messing up and having the world throwing stones at me."

His nose wrinkles as if something stinks. "Dude, whining's not a good look on you."

"And this orange is?" I flick the lapel.

He shrugs and tilts his head to the side while giving my getup a onceover. "It's in your color wheel, actually."

I'm pretty sure he just made that up and don't care enough to call him out on it. "Just leave me already." I point toward the right, knowing the door is somewhere in that direction.

"I'll be by tomorrow to check on you." He turns to leave.

"Drew, thanks for everything." I wait for him to meet my eyes before adding, "And thank you for always showing up when no one else will."

The sucker stick wobbles between his lips as Drew raises a fist between the bars. I bump mine against his, a silent oath we share to always have each other's backs.

Even though his eyes are glassy with tears, he ticks his chin up and strolls away like he hasn't a care in the world.

Chapter Eighteen

Bellamy

The small conference room in the back of the church is filled with too many frowning faces. The Church Committee, made up of mostly elders, called this emergency meeting about Lee. Being the church secretary, I'm required to sit in and take notes, but we all know I'm here for more than that this time. The photos Mia and Neena showed up to walk me through last night flicker through my mind, sending the heat of my cheeks up several degrees. With my eyes glued to the blank notepad on the table in front of me to dodge everyone's scrutiny, the headlines keep popping in my head like flashing billboards.

House Arrest or House Party
Bad-Boy Lee Sutton's New Play Toy
Valley Church Lets the Devil In

Many others on the same lines, and every one of them are accompanied with a photo that includes me. Barely able to swallow, I have a sickening feeling that this meeting will include a request for my resignation. I wouldn't blame them one bit, and I'm prepared for it.

"Chase, would you like to give us a summary of actual facts about what has been going on with Lee Sutton…" Mr. Garcia's eyes dart to me over the top of his glasses before he returns them to Chase. "And anything else that has been going on around here."

Chase passes a stack of papers to each member and then gives me one. "The top paper is the house arrest agreement we had with Judge Pruitt. Underneath it is Lee's service hours log. You'll notice he completed the required hours a few weeks ago and has been doing more out of the goodness of his heart." One of the members snorts at that comment. "It's the truth, Mr. Jenkins," Chase retorts. "You asked for facts. The next page is a summary of money Lee has spent out of his own pocket for the church. He's done a few things that I'm unable to find out the total, but it's roughly a hundred grand that I'm aware of."

"Was this part of the house arrest agreement?" Mr. Garcia returns to the top page and begins scanning it for the answer that's not there.

"No, sir. Lee did that on his own. Just as he's done with the continuation of service hours."

"And how does Bellamy come in to this?" Mr. Jenkins asks, not beating around the bush.

The room is warming at a considerable rate and my heart starts to race.

"She has assisted me with assigning Lee service projects and supervising him." Chase shuffles through his papers but before he can continue the members make it clear where their concerns lie by asking several rapid-fire questions about the elephant in the room.

Mr. Jenkins reins them all in before addressing Chase like I'm not in the room. "We've reviewed numerous images this morning that are highly questionable, Chase. So you can stop tiptoeing around. We want the truth."

"The truth is Bellamy and Lee have grown close during his stay here. It didn't happen for quite a while. I see nothing wrong with that."

"*Nothing* wrong with a naked criminal frolicking around in the waterfall on church property with the church secretary looking like she's about to join him?" Mr. Morton speaks for the first time, and I so wish he hadn't.

Chase clears his throat. "Bellamy, would you care to explain that?"

"I didn't realize he would be in there washing... I was shocked finding him there, but then I got ahold of him about it and left!" I'm so embarrassed and mad that tears plop from my eyes before I can contain them. "I've never been one to buy gossip magazines or watch celebrity news, but I've caught headlines over the years and pictures that go with them... I'm ashamed to admit that I believed them because a picture doesn't lie, right?" I sniffle and bat the tears off my scalding cheeks. "Now I realize how a picture can be misinterpreted. I, in no way, did anything inappropriate with Lee Sutton. I kissed him, yes. I've even told him I love him... Something I didn't think I'd ever feel for a man again after losing Beau."

"Bellamy—" Chase begins, but I interrupt.

"I do admit that my actions reflect poorly on Valley Church. I would never intentionally do that. For that I apologize..." I take a staggered breath and pull the envelope from my purse. "And I'll save you the trouble of asking. Here's my official resignation."

"No, Bellamy, that's not what we're here seeking today." Chase shakes his head, but when no one else at the table backs him on that, I hand him the envelope and walk out.

As the door closes, the men erupt in argument. I continue down the hall that feels like a tunnel with no light at the end of it, stop in my office for my wedding picture, and head out. After placing the photo in the truck, I go over to the garage to see about gathering No-tail and his food bowls.

Taking a fortifying breath, I open the door only to have some invisible force knock the breath right back out of me. The place is void of Lee's personal belongings, including No-tail and the life we had been building together.

The impact sends me to my knees, clutching my stomach and crying so hard it produces no sound.

****

I'm not even sure when or how I picked myself up off the floor of the garage, but I did and even managed to get home in one piece to start packing. The same numbness that followed me home that night from the morgue has shown back up, following me room to room like a heavy shadow as I gather things to take with me. Losing Beau was detrimental, and I know if I lie down in my bedroom and give in to grief once again, I won't recover this time around.

Not knowing any other option but to put as much space between me and another loss, I pause long enough in my frenzied packing to book a flight to Washington. Without taking a look back, I shut the lights off and leave like a thief in the night.

I make it past the gate and board the plane without incident, but have to contend with a few passengers on a repetitive pattern of stealing glances at me. By the time the plane touches down, I've had enough of the looks and can't unload and find my next gate fast enough.

If I thought enduring looks on the first flight were bad, I'd been sadly mistaken. Two hours. That's the length of my layover, and it starts with me going to one of those kiosks for a cup of coffee and maybe a book or magazine to read. Before I order the coffee, my eyes land on a succession of magazines with me splashed all over the covers.

Face hot and throat closing, I scoot a little closer and find a set of pictures I'd not seen yet. The first one is me leaving out the garage with a very sleep-rumpled Lee following behind me. The next one is him pulling me in for a kiss. The last is me walking backwards and offering him a flirty wave. Truly, the display looks like I'm sneaking out after spending the night with him, when I know for fact that wasn't what happened that morning.

Ashamed and furious at myself, even though it didn't happen, I turn away without purchasing anything. Hanging my head, I hitch my bag onto my shoulder and head to my next gate.

Not three entire steps are made before I hear my name being called from behind me. Then, as if a swarm of bees have attacked, I'm surrounded by a fury of cameras and very inappropriate questions. It causes such a scene that security ends up escorting me to a private lounge to wait until time to board the flight that will finish getting me away from Lee Sutton and the circus that seems to be his real life.

While waiting, I give in and do a Google search on my phone to see exactly who this man is I've been *fornicating* with, as some of the headlines put it. After wading past the newest headlines that all include me, a wave of nausea hits me followed by acute jealousy with the discovery.

Photo after photo of woman after woman in compromising situations with Lee are displayed on the screen, making me wonder if I'd been nothing but a fool to think what we had was anything special. Was this offensive behavior the reason for his celebrity status and not that of his company? Maybe I'd lived a sheltered life in my back office at church, but I can make no sense of what's happening in our world where it seems vulgarity merits fame. It's as if people feed off of others' sins and failures like rabid addicts. It's sickening.

One thing is for certain, I want no part in it.

"Ma'am, it's time to board." The security guard escorts me to the gate, keeping the hecklers at arm's length, but does nothing to protect my ears from the inappropriate questions and the cruel comments. By the time I'm slumped in my plane seat, the tears have started and continue until my head is pounding and the sky outside fades to night.

Chapter Nineteen

Lee

Surrounded by dark wood walls, wood tables and chairs, I get a sense of déjà vu. This time the aches from the wreck and the effects of alcohol withdrawals aren't consuming me like bees buzzing around my brain. This time, completely sober and of sound mind, I have nothing to focus on but the problem at hand. And if Lance is correct, that will look like a year behind bars for me. Three days of that has been enough. Three hundred and sixty-five more sounds like a death sentence.

"You may be seated," the bailiff states.

As we all sit, there's commotion behind me, and I figure it's last-minute reporters shoving their way in to claim a pound of me. I do as I've always done, and only give them my back. I unbutton the Tom Ford suit jacket, even though Lance instructed Drew to bring the cheaper one to the jail. He told Lance he could shove it up his we-all-know-what and that I would at least be comfortable during this court appearance.

Drew got another fist bump for that.

"Mr. Sutton, seems you've been quite busy since our last visit back in July." Judge Pruitt frowns at the file, squinting at it like it makes no sense. I'm with him on that.

Since sitting in the cell for the last three days, I've concluded life is made up of nothing but nonsense. Even when I'm keeping my nose clean for a change, stupid stuff still trips me.

"You have anything to say for yourself?" Pruitt asks, his beady eyes peering at me over the top of his ill-fitted glasses. It's on the tip of my tongue to recommend my optometrist to him, but I tamp it down.

"No sense in wasting your time, sir. I'm sure your mind's made up. Just get on with it." I motion with a flicked wrist. From Lance's defeated sigh and the judge's hard glare, my truth isn't welcome here today, but it's all I got.

A throat clears behind me. "Judge, I'd like a word with you first."

I peer over my shoulder, knowing it's Jeb, but I'm surprised that each mahogany bench is filled with Valley Church members instead of nosy media. Pop catches my eye from the back row and tips his head at me. I return the gesture and move my attention to the judge before I start blubbering.

"This isn't how this works, Jeb, and you know it." Judge Pruitt yanks his glasses off and tosses them on top of my thick file. Those dumb pages are still creased and wrinkled.

"Well, it should be," Clarence pipes in, grunting as his rotund body manages to stand beside a much taller and leaner Jeb. "The system is hogwash anymore. This here boy has mended his wrongs and you need to hear about it. That picture taken of our Bellamy riding around on Lee's bike... Where's the pictures of him riding us around that same day? And on church property at that!"

The Men's Group is great, but I don't want them to get in trouble on my behalf. I lean over to Lance and whisper harshly, "Get them to sit down."

Pruitt sits back in his leather seat, rolls his eyes to the ceiling, and then fixes his eyes on the men standing up for me. "I could have you both arrested for contempt and obstruction of justice."

"Yeah, you could." Harvey slowly stands and joins the others. "But you know what's right is right, no matter how many of them rules is rewritten by idiots thinking they know the law while turning their backs on the word of God."

Oh, dang. I'm new at this, but know no court system wants God to be a part of it anymore. "Sit down," I hiss over my shoulder, but the old men don't seem to have their hearing aids turned up.

"Yoo-hoo, Cletus," Ms. Mary from the Ladies of Faith waves at the judge. "Honey, we need to talk about how this fine young man has been looking out for the shut-ins and those poor neglected souls at the nursing home. I do believe your Uncle Davis is one of them. Shame on your for not taking better care of your kin." The gray-headed lady tsks, and I turn around and slump in my chair.

"I'm gonna rot in prison, ain't I?" I mutter under my breath to Lance.

The judge jabs a finger behind me. "Y'all turning my courtroom into a circus and—"

"If you'd just listen," Harvey pleads.

"Lance, you and Sutton in my chambers. *Now.*" Pruitt nearly growls as he shoots to his feet and leaves his bench.

Once we're in his chambers, which is just a fancy word for office, Pruitt settles on a couch and pins me with a glare. "Tell me what you did wrong?"

"What I did wrong?" I place a foot on my knee and get comfortable in the wingback chair. "I got myself smashed by downing a fifth of Jack, climbed on my bike, drove drunk, and wrecked."

"Lee," Lance blurts, but I ignore him.

"I took advantage of women. Wasted a lot of life and a ton of money on stupidity."

"And recently?" Pruitt's bushy white eyebrows shoot up over the top of his glasses, looking like fuzzy caterpillars.

I lower my gaze to meet his dark eyes and speak earnestly. "Recently, I've been working on righting my wrongs, putting the gifts God has given me to good use. I ain't gone about it perfectly, but I've done my best. I have no regrets in any of it, except maybe the paparazzi taking liberties of snagging pictures on private property and figuring out how to use them falsely. Valley Church doesn't deserve to be dragged into my mess. They've been nothing but good to me." After giving him a measured look, I lower my head, feeling worn down to the point of giving up.

"I know that already. And if your *witnesses* didn't interrupt, you'd know that." Pruitt sighs. "Pastor Chase McCoy provided me with your community service log, the hours you've volunteered over what was required, and most importantly, the security camera footage that provides proof of you riding many people around the designated area of the parking lot on your bike. He also provided camera footage from the waterfall area."

My head pops up from studying my lap. "Huh?"

"The entire church property is monitored with security cameras. You didn't think Chase would just let you loose to do whatever, did you?"

I'm slightly offended, yet beyond relieved. I know those cameras may have caught some pretty personal moments, but it shows I did nothing to violate my parole. "So what does that mean?"

"It means I have the decision to make on whether to send you back to Valley Church for five more months to finish out your sentence."

"I'm willing."

"I know."

Pruitt fills us in on what he thinks is best, and I have no other choice but to accept it.

Chapter Twenty

Bellamy

A dense fog blankets the world outside the enclosed porch, giving a false sense that nothing exists past it. If only that were the case.

"Honey, did you hear me?"

Blinking out of my own fog, I focus on the cup of spiced tea in my hand. It's my mom's favorite, but it reminds me too much of Lee so all I can do is hold it. "I'm sorry, Momma, what was that?" I look over to her when she lets out a heavy sigh, and I wish I hadn't. Looking into her golden eyes is like staring at a reflection of my grief. "Please stop looking at me like that."

"It's hard not to. You've been here for three weeks and not even my Christmas feast yesterday cheered you up." Momma reaches over and wraps her hand around my forearm. "It's worse than before."

"What is?"

"You shut down after Beau passed, but you somehow managed to at least pretend to be going through the motions of living. This time you're not even trying to do that."

"I don't have the strength this time..." After I made it safely into my parent's house, I shut down and allowed the numbness to seep through me. Shutting the world out was pretty easy when I tossed my phone in the bay. I'd had my fill of obscene messages and voicemails offering me even more obscene amounts of money for tell-all interviews before the taxi even arrived to Momma and Daddy's townhouse.

"But… Please don't take this the wrong way and think I'm being cruel, but Lee isn't dead."

I know she isn't being cruel, but it stings just the same. Feeling the pressure of another headache beginning, I rub my forehead and release a groan. "It's not that simple."

"Why not?"

Not wanting to go another round about all the reasons, I shake my head and go back to staring at my cooling tea. Eventually, I mumble, "I was so naïve. I knew who Lee Sutton was, but I had no idea he was such a hot gossip topic in the celebrity world. And in not knowing, I made a fool of myself and my church."

"Chase has reassured you that's not the case." Momma sets her cup on the small patio table and takes mine and does the same.

Chase is the only contact in my new phone, and he's enough. Daily texts and calls from him alone fill up my voicemail. He was quick to let me know Judge Pruitt granted Lee an early release on a one-year probation. I've wondered what Lee has been doing since being released, but have managed to tamp down my curiosity enough to stay away from searching his name on the Internet.

"Bellamy, did you hear me?" Momma catches me drifting away in my thoughts again.

"You didn't see the Church Committee at that meeting. They made it clear Chase was the only one who felt that way. After seeing those pictures, I really don't blame them."

"So, what's your plan?"

I shrug. "I guess I need to start looking for a job and maybe a place to live."

"Honey, your daddy and I have loved having you here, but clearly your home is in Tennessee."

"But I'm so embarrassed. Those photos made me look like another one of Lee's hookups with loose morals."

"So you're going to stay here in hiding and let what others think about you rob you of a life waiting to be claimed?"

Lee hasn't contacted me, and I'm pretty sure he could have found me if he wanted to, so I'm not so sure what life there is waiting for me to claim. "I don't know what to do, okay?"

"Just think about it before making permanent decisions. Your daddy and I will support you in whatever you choose."

Momma leaves it at that and we spend the rest of the day putting Christmas decorations away, only leaving the tree for another day or two. I go to bed early like I have since arriving, reasoning that the quicker I go to sleep the quicker I can escape my reality. Dumb thinking, because most nights are spent staring into the darkness.

Tonight, I settle under the covers and prop up on the pillows to do some job searches in the area, although I have no clue as to what I'm even looking for. After skimming over a few listings for receptionists and executive assistants that sound too much like my old life, I move the search to florists and bakeries and then search for any bookstore listings. Those are always popular jobs heroines seem to have in the books I've read lately—the fictional world may have some insight on career happiness. The world must not think so, because there are no listings for those anywhere close to here.

I'm about to give up and start staring off into the void of night when a text message from Chase pops up.

You need to watch this.

The message has a link attached to it, indicating it's from a popular nightly talk show. I'm tempted to ignore it, but he texts in all capital letters.

DO NOT IGNORE ME. ENOUGH!

Chase has never shouted at me, much less through text, so I tap the link and steel myself for what I know won't be anything pleasant.

The beautiful, middle-aged hostess welcomes viewers to the show before introducing her guest. "Tonight, we have an exclusive with the one and only Lee Sutton." The camera zooms out to include the chair beside her.

Dressed in dark jeans, a white Henley topped with his worn leather jacket, and those signature boots on his feet, Lee looks like the famous bad-boy the world has made him out to be.

"Lee, seems you've been living one interesting year and making quite a few headlines lately." The hostess gives him a coy smile.

Lee runs a hand through his freshly tousled hair in that hipster style he pulls off so well. Even though he is the picture of confident aloofness in such a raw, sensual package, the neatly trimmed stubble on his jaw doesn't hide the muscle flexing just underneath it.

When he remains quiet, she softly laughs. "Oh, come on, Lee. Care to explain?"

"I've made a lot of poor choices in the last few years. They finally caught up with me." Lee is blunt for the next few minutes, going through the wreck, arrest, and sentencing. He answers her questions in a clipped tone but doesn't beat around the bush, either.

"And would you like to share some details about this foundation you've started?" The line of questioning makes it's easy to tell they have some sort of agreement on how the interview would go. *Confess your sins and then get a plug in for your foundation.*

"Yes. During my stay at Valley Church, my guardians Chase McCoy and his sister-in-law, Bellamy, opened my eyes to how my actions produce consequences that affect others. Bellamy in particular, whose husband was killed by a drunk driver, inspired me to form a rehabilitation program to help people like the man who killed her husband. Witnessing her work through forgiving the guy made me realize, no matter if we deserve it or not, we all need forgiveness."

"That's quite honorable of Ms. McCoy."

"It is. She's an amazing woman, and in no way deserves what the media has said about her."

"But those pictures? You know I have to ask you about your relationship with her and how unethical it looks."

"Kate, you've been a witness to this social media disease long enough to know a picture can tell a thousand *lies*."

She waves a manicured hand at him. "Well, Lee, here's your opportunity to tell a thousand *truths*."

"First truth is, I respect and love Bellamy too much to sit here and tell you details of our private life. She's been through too much already, and what the gossip rags have done is take something pure and probably ruined it. And the last truth is that I've never been in love before, but now that I am, I realize it's more important than making bank."

"What do you mean by that?"

"It means this will be my last TV appearance. I've also ended my professional relationship with my agent and have resolved all contracts with the show. I'm done after this with the public. I won't be a puppet in their sick game of watch the celebrity fall anymore and I won't expose my loved ones to it, either."

"Are you blaming social media for your fall?" She quickly asks, like she knows exactly where to deliver the jab.

"Not at all. My actions are all on me. But they're responsible for taking it and twisting it, making people foam at the mouth to see the train wreck. Word of advice to the world..." Lee turns and looks directly into the camera. "Find something worthy with integrity to follow. I've been a poor example. For that I'm sorry."

Lee tips his head to Kate, indicating he's done.

"Well, folks, you've heard it here first. Lee Sutton, good luck to you. For more information on his foundation, visit our website and tune in after..."

The interview clip concludes, and I immediately restart it just as Momma walks into the bedroom. I try to shut it off, but she reaches over and catches my hand.

"What is this?"

I'm too choked up to explain, so I angle the phone and let her see for herself.

Once it concludes, she gasps. "Oh my goodness. I do believe that man is truly in love with you."

I dry my cheek with the sleeve of my shirt and nod. "I think you're right."

We both watch the interview again before she heads to bed, and then I continue watching it until the battery icon on the phone turns red.

****

A few days have slowly passed since watching the interview more times than I care to admit. It made me realize, if Lee was brave enough to be subjected to that interview, then I can be brave enough to walk through this airport with my head held high. I can go home to face the music. Momma was right. I know the truth, Lee knows the truth, and more importantly, God knows the truth. We did nothing wrong but fall in love at perhaps the worst moment in time. No matter, it happened, so it's time to go home and see what happens next.

Surprisingly, I make it to Tennessee without one run-in, making it clear that the paparazzi sharks are only out for blood and stop circling when there is none. Glad to be considered boring and unpopular again, I go home and try to gather enough bravado to attend church service in the morning.

Even after a restless night of praying and pep-talking myself, apprehension follows me into the sanctuary. It quickly dissolves when the first ones to greet me are the members of the Church Committee. I'm offered side-hugs and apologies and my job back. I accept the apologies, but I'm not sure what I want to do about that just yet, so I simply nod and hug.

Finally, when the welcoming hymn begins, I am left to escape to my pew. Picking up the hymnal, I flip to the proper page and try not to be too disappointed to be sitting alone. Not even a verse in, several people move over and join me to completely fill the pew. I offer a smile to each one even though the one I want to see the most isn't among them. I wonder if I'm being naïve again to think Lee would still come to church services even after he'd been released on probation.

After service, many come up and invite me to Sunday dinner. Mia Calder is one of them, and I'm barely able to get away from her, but manage to do so with promises of taking her up on the offer next Sunday.

I spend the afternoon dusting, washing linens, and making a grocery list. By the time that's done, I brave pulling out my laptop to do a job search. While waiting for it to power up, I pour myself a glass of water and have a seat at the table.

The deep rumble of a motor rolls up to the house. I set the glass down, sloshing water on the newly waxed table. I grab a towel to mop up the beads of water, then hurry to the door and wait until I hear the motorcycle shut off before opening the door.

Standing in my small yard, Lee's dressed similar to what he wore in the interview. It's dreamlike to see him outside the setting of church. I have the overwhelming urge to plow down the steps and go touch him to confirm he's real, but manage to tamp that down and stay rooted to the porch.

When he remains quiet, I blurt, "You weren't at church."

"And you haven't been there in three weeks." The deep timbre of his voice reaches me, weakening my knees. "Gavin and Gatlin took part in a program at their church today. I would've let you know if I had your number. I didn't even have a clue you were back until about an hour ago."

"You took No-tail." The defensive words come out like an accusation.

Lee slowly blinks as his head tilts to the side. "You never made a public claim on him. How was I supposed to know you wanted him?"

"If I had, you would have let me keep him?"

He places his hands on the seat of the bike and leans against it. The movement stretches the white thermal shirt across his chest. His presence is so larger than life, it sucks the air right out of me. "That's all you ever had to do, Belle, to claim *anything* you wanted."

"Even you?" I ask before stopping myself.

A slow smile crosses his gorgeous face. "Even me."

We hold each other's gaze for a long pause to let that truth settle between us.

What's been eating at me ever since I left comes bubbling up the back of my throat in a choked sob. "I'm sorry I was a chicken and ran away. I should have stayed by your side and been stronger and—"

"No." He holds a palm up. "No need for apologizing. I didn't want you here."

I flinch.

"Because you've been through enough. I never want to be the cause of you going through anything else like that. If you wouldn't have left, I was working on having Drew kidnap you away, so thank you for preventing us from committing another crime." He winks one of those brilliant blue eyes at me, righting my world in a way I never thought possible. "I missed you like mad, babe."

"Me too. I'm so proud of you. You know that, right?" I bat an escaped tear away.

"I missed your liquid-gold eyes. And your sass. And how you always make me feel worthy."

"Because you are worthy, Lee. I'm glad the world has finally been able to see the true you."

He hitches a thumb over his shoulder. "That world doesn't matter to me. Just my world here that I've discovered in the last year." His voice grows thicker than before. "You wanna know what else I've missed?"

Knowing my own voice would probably come out all squeaky, I simply nod.

"I miss our Sunday afternoons together." Lee pushes off the bike and saunters up the porch steps, stopping on one just below me. It brings us to eye level and makes it easier to smooth my hand along his jaw, feeling it flex underneath my touch. He turns his head, places a kiss to my palm, and says, "I want our Sundays back."

I want to tell him I want every part of us back, but whisper instead, "Okay."

"Whattaya say we go for a ride?"

I agree again, and within a short amount of time, I'm properly bundled up and holding on to Lee as he drives us through the mountains.

The ride begins there and continues each Sunday afternoon for several weeks as Lee slowly introduces me to his world outside of house arrest. He takes me to his shop, which is more like a giant plaza with a merchandise store and small snack shop up front and numerous design studios in the back. Another Sunday, I find myself at a small cemetery where his brother is buried while Lee tells me about some adolescent adventures they shared and then takes me to the house he grew up in.

It's like we are on a redo with learning each other. We go out to eat, attend church together, and all the other normal things couples do. It's refreshing after our first go was so unconventional. We have long conversations on the phone at night with me pouring out my apprehensions on going back to the church and Lee being supportive of what I decide, going as far as offering me a job at his shop. But the more I've talked to him about it, the more I realize Valley Church is my home in more than one way. My heart says it's time to let go of my humiliation and go back.

Late February shows up and gives us a mild day with plenty of sunshine, so I hurry home after church and change into my standard riding outfit of jeans and a hoodie. I don't have to wait long before the mean rumble of Lee's bike announces his arrival. It's no less thrilling than the first time I heard it, and I don't wait for it to shut off before I'm out the door and down the steps. After placing a quick kiss on his cheek, I climb on and settle in for whatever adventure he has up his sleeve for the day.

Today's adventure leads to a gate with a long driveway behind it. I'm pretty sure it leads to a home he has yet to show me. We've just gotten used to him spending time in my home, so I've seen no reason to rush this part either. After Lee opens the gate by remote, he slowly drives us up the winding road until coming to a halt in front of a rustic log cabin. Well, more like a log mansion.

Stunned, I stay seated on the bike and peer up at the beautiful home set amongst towering trees and comforting isolation. "Wow, Lee... This is... wow."

He offers me his hand and pulls me to standing. "I take that as you liking it?"

"Liking? No, I love it."

Lee opens the giant front door and motions me inside to an open floor plan. A massive stone island is the only thing that separates the wood-dressed living room from the kitchen, which makes it easy to pull my attention straight to the two sets of French doors that lead to a sprawling deck off the back. A few steps in that direction reveal an enormous pool and spa.

"I can't believe there are no pictures online of this place. It's stunning."

Lee joins me by the French doors. "You been checking me out online, babe?"

"Who hasn't checked the famous Lee Sutton out online?" I bat my eyelashes, full of tease, before growing serious. "I figured if I was going to give this relationship with you a go, I needed to rip the Band-Aid off and research what I was getting myself into. The only thing I couldn't unearth about you was pictures of where you lived, except for images of the gate out front."

"Because that's as far as they've ever been allowed to get." Lee shoves his hands into his back pockets and peers down at me. "I needed a place just for me where no media or my stupidity has touched. It's my haven."

"And Drew's?"

"Yeah. It was his, but I've found him a private place of his own a few miles from here. Just got him moved this week."

"Why did you move him?"

"Because my plan is to share this home with you. Can't do that privately with the punk in our backyard."

I turn from the majestic view outside to find him giving me a heated smile. "I'm not shacking up with you, Lee Sutton."

His eyes squint, drawing his brows together. "Well, why not?"

"Because!" I try to shove him away when he wraps an arm around my waist and pulls me close.

"Will this change your mind?" Lee produces a ring from his pocket and shows it to me.

"That's a man's wedding band."

"I know what it is, Belle." He flips my palm up and drops the ring in it. "As I recall, you stole a ring from me a while back. I think it's only fair for you to replace it."

"This is unconventional," I quip, gazing down at the titanium band that's as weighty as what he's proposing.

"It's been our style from the very beginning, hasn't it?"

He's absolutely right, so I give in and slide the ring on his finger as I place my lips to his and kiss him with a fierceness I didn't even know I was capable of. It barely registers when he picks me up and settles me on top of the giant kitchen island. Wrapping me tightly in his arms, Lee takes over the kiss until my world spins.

I end it with a good bit of reluctance and barely breathe his name. "Lee…"

"Just kissing…" He groans so deeply it ricochets throughout my entire body. "I promise… until we decide to say I do, just good old-fashioned kissing. Okay?" He nuzzles my neck, feeling anything but old-fashioned.

When I say nothing but let out a whimper, he pulls back slightly. "You good with that, Belle? You gonna let me marry you, right?"

Accepting the unconventional proposal, I murmur past a happy sob, "Yes."

Lee holds true to his word and lays some really nice old-fashioned kissing on me. I'm amazed that God took the ruins of both our lives and reworked tragedy and regrets into a beauty no one but the two of us would recognize.

And it would have never happened until we decided to let God have all those wrongs to create the redemption he had in store.

Epilogue

Lee

Flat on my back, surrounded by inky skies and a giant full moon looming right above me, I can hardly catch my breath. It's my chest's fault. It's too tight. I pull my hand free and rub the center of it.

"Are you okay?"

I turn my head in Bellamy's direction, considering her question, and notice the concern in those bewitching golden eyes. I've had that question asked time and time again, and I have always answered it with a lie. I'd bow up and say everything was fine even though my world was usually in crumbles from some asinine choice I'd made or a terrible circumstance I had no control over. But this is Bellamy, the one person I've never lied to and don't want to start now.

"Lee?" she asks when I keep silent and just stare.

"No, Belle. I'm not okay." I stop rubbing my chest where my blessings and happiness swell to the point of overwhelming me and roll to my side beside her on the quilt we've spread out in the backyard. "I'm more than okay. I'm beyond fine."

The worry vanishes and her beautiful face lights up with a smile. "You most certainly are *fine*."

That saucy tease has me rolling again and pinning my wife underneath me, claiming a lingering kiss that I know is more than okay and beyond fine. She doesn't put up any resistance either. Funny how that's changed drastically since the first time I tried pulling this stunt with her.

"What are you grinning about?" Bellamy asks against my lips.

"You, babe, you make me so dang happy. And I sure am glad you don't fry my face when I try making a pass at you anymore." I press another kiss to her lips when they join mine in curling up in a grin.

A familiar rustling sound has us both freezing like two teenagers caught making out. Holding my breath, I look over to check the portable monitor at the edge of the quilt. The movement on the screen stops, but I keep my eyes glued to it while dropping a kiss on the tip of Bellamy's nose.

Bellamy giggles. "Is she awake?"

I keep watching for further movement but there is none. "Nah. She's just like her momma. Can't even get still while sleeping." I tsk and lean down for another kiss.

At sixteen months old and looking like a mini Bellamy, Harley Sutton already owns me. I never thought my heart had the capacity to love one woman, let alone two, but the moment the nurse handed my daughter to me I was smitten.

"Let's make another baby." I unfasten the top button on Bellamy's jeans. "We have some more rooms to fill."

She quietly laughs like I'm joking but I'm not, so I spend the next long stretch of this date night proving how serious I really am.

Later, after we're both spent, I roll over to give her some breathing room and go back to staring at the star-studded sky. It's a warm spring night so I'm in no hurry to conclude our date.

Bellamy reaches over to hold my hand and lets out a soft sigh. It's one of my favorite sounds because that sound tells me all is right in my wife's world. "I love this backyard."

I follow her gaze over toward the pergola the Men's Group helped me construct for our wedding two summers ago. We exchanged vows underneath it and I intend to live the rest of my life by them. Chase sat us down and actually explained what each part meant, saying he wouldn't be responsible for us having any misconceptions.

To have and to hold from this day forward,
For better or for worse,
For richer, for poorer,
In sickness and in health,
To love and to cherish;
From this day forward until death do us part.

Before we signed the marriage license that day, I felt we'd already tried out most of those vows. Bellamy had definitely seen me at my worst while I was having alcohol withdrawals and angry at the world. She was pretty broken in spirit at the time herself. She was there to help me mend from the accident even though my sorry tail didn't deserve it. Bellamy survived the *death do us part* one time already, so I'm honored she's willing to risk enduring that vow again for me. Truthfully, it hurts too bad to think about that part being fulfilled myself, but I'm not missing out on this gift by being a coward.

Our vows cover the hard parts, but they also cover the really good stuff too, and I'm all about fulfilling them. Case in point, this private picnic and pulling my wife into my arms to keep my vow of cherishing her, loving her, holding her.

Best decision of my life.

Until I Decide Playlist

"Natural" by Imagine Dragons
"Heavydirtysoul" by twenty one pilots
"Glycerine" by Bush
"Feel Invincible" by Skillet
"Something Beautiful" by NEEDTOBREATHE
"The Distance" by Cake
"Hallelujah" by Panic! At the Disco
"Everybody Talks" by Neon Trees
"When Mercy Found Me" by Rhett Walker Band
"One and Only" by Adele
"You Say" by Lauren Daigle
"Hold Us Together" by Matt Maher

If you enjoyed this southern romance, T.I. recommends you check out *Written in the Stars* by Christina Coryell. It's one of her favorites!

Written in the Stars
(an excerpt)

Something was wrong.

Holly knew it with every fiber of her being, like that weird sixth sense she had that told her when lightning bugs would begin illuminating the dusky sky. The color of the atmosphere around her would change ever so slightly, and she would start anxiously watching the grass for the little boogers to begin darting up into the air, putting on a show.

Whatever this was, it had nothing to do with lightning bugs.

If someone were to break in through the back door, her dog Skittles would destroy the place with his weak bladder. Not that a person would try to pull anything roundabout her neck of the woods, where everybody and their brother packed heat. Her eyes nervously darted to the shotgun above her doorframe, held up by strategically placed nails. She'd never used the gun for anything other than taking out that snake lurking around the premises, waiting for her dog to get a little too close. She wasn't too keen on using it now if the need presented itself, although it had nothing to do with her aim. That was top notch. If anyone doubted it, they could ask the snake.

This wasn't an ordinary snake in the grass though. Whatever it was, she sensed it in her bones, and she didn't like it one bit.

Nobody would get in through the back door, she assured herself. She'd locked it on the knob and the little chain up above, which she knew because she'd already checked it twice. And Skittles wouldn't be tearing up the place either—the little Havanese was tucked away in his crate for safe keeping.

Even the zipper on her jeans was secure...she'd checked that more than once too. Most recently while she peered at her reflection in the mirror for at least the tenth time, but she looked down once more for good measure. Yep, right where it needed to be.

Her eyes darted back up to meet themselves in the mirror. It must have been nerves, that was all. Of course she'd have a hard time following through when it actually came down to it.

"You can do this," she whispered, smoothing the ends of her shoulder-length blond hair. She couldn't remember the last time she had taken so much time on her appearance, or the last time she looked quite so pulled together, for that matter. The center of her bottom lip shimmered a bit when she twisted, the light meeting the sparkle in her lip gloss.

With a determined nod at her reflection, she grabbed her purse, took one last look around the room, and crossed to the front door. But before she fully committed to stepping out into the night, Holly Christian drew open the drawer of the beaten-up desk, slid the diamond ring off her left hand, and tucked it safely inside.

Christina Coryell is a USA Today bestselling author of real-life contemporary fiction, mingling honesty with humor and characters who could be friends. A resident of small-town southwest Missouri, where she lives with her husband and two children, she does most of her scribbling in unorthodox places and with lots of noise in the background.

About the Author

Bestselling author T.I. Lowe is living her dream as a writer. She knows she's just getting started and has many more stories to tell. A wife and mother and active in her church community, she resides in coastal South Carolina with her family.

For more information, visit tilowe.com.